ALL HE S[...]
DO WAS POINT HIS FINGER

He pointed his right index finger like a pistol. Suddenly a glowing red sight ring was superimposed on the ground below him. He centered the pip in the ring on his target and squeezed his right trigger finger, hoping that there wasn't some kind of interlock that prevented the laser from firing so close to its own control facility.

There wasn't, and the laser fired.

The first shot hit at the front of the hostile formation. The effect of the laser beam was like an artillery shell landing in the middle of them. There was no shrapnel, but the intense heat caused trees to explode and rocks to burst as the water inside them was instantly turned into superheated steam.

The Brazilians dove for cover, but there was no escaping the Finger of God. Rosemont shifted his point of aim and fired again. The beam caught one of the Brazilians directly, and he burst into flames. His comrades recoiled in horror and looked at the heavens. The laser touched down again, and they broke and ran. Dropping their weapons, they scattered into the brush as fast as they could run.

WARKEEP

2030

FINGER OF GOD
Michael Kasner

A GOLD EAGLE BOOK FROM
WORLDWIDE ®

TORONTO • NEW YORK • LONDON
AMSTERDAM • PARIS • SYDNEY • HAMBURG
STOCKHOLM • ATHENS • TOKYO • MILAN
MADRID • WARSAW • BUDAPEST • AUCKLAND

First edition November 1993

ISBN 0-373-62017-9

FINGER OF GOD

This edition published by arrangement with Harlequin Enterprises B.V.

® and TM are trademarks of the publisher. Trademarks indicated
with ® are registered in the United States Patent and Trademark
Office, the Canadian Trade Marks Office and in other countries.

Printed in U.S.A.

FINGER OF GOD

1

The Amazon jungle—6 November 2030 A.D.

The sleek black cat stopped in midstride and sniffed the air again. The smell of day-old blood was enticing, and the tip of her tail twitched. It had been days since she had fed, and her greedy nursing cubs were sapping her strength. But along with the smell of blood, the air carried the hated scent of human. It was a stale scent, however, free of the rank stench of fresh man-sweat.

Her hunger driving her, the panther moved closer, her ears scanning for the slightest noise. Soundlessly she broke through the brush into a large clearing among the towering trees of the rain forest.

The clearing in the jungle was man-made, and it had been made recently. The raw stumps were still oozing sap, and the trunks of the trees were lying where they had fallen. The limbs had been trimmed off from some of the trunks to make them into logs.

Scattered in between the fallen trees lay the bodies of six men, clad in khaki tropical uniforms with the blue-and-white shoulder insignia of the United Nations. A large green-and-blue patch sewn on the right pocket of their uniform jackets proclaimed that they had been serving with the UN Environmental Protection Service, the Green Police.

For the past three years, Brazil had been under UN sanctions designed to halt further destruction of the Amazon rain forests. These measures had been taken when the government proved unable to stop the cutting and burning on their own. The proud Brazilians did not welcome UN interference in what they saw as purely an internal affair, but they had had no say in the matter. Globally the survival of the remaining rain forest was seen as more important than mere national sovereignty.

The big cat didn't particularly like the taste of human flesh and she preferred her meat freshly killed, but she was too hungry to be picky today. If anything, cats are the ultimate pragmatists. Purring like a furry chain saw, the big cat crouched beside the body and began feeding.

When her ears brought her the faint sound of a human flying machine rapidly approaching, the cat stopped in midbite, her ears pivoting to pinpoint the sound. She growled low in her throat and backed away from the corpse, her tail twitching and the fur between her shoulders raised.

She did not want to leave before she had finished devouring this unexpected bounty, but she knew the danger of the flying machine. Were it not for the fact that the humans were approaching so quickly, she would have dragged her meal up into a tree for safekeeping until she could get back to finish it. But her belly was almost full now, and she could nurse her cubs again.

As the chopper's rotor changed pitch when the pilot flared out for a landing in the clearing, the big cat disappeared back into the jungle like a fading shadow.

The man who stepped out of the chopper wore the blue beret and crisp khaki uniform of a UN observer. The pips on his epaulets proclaimed him to be the UN rank equivalent to an army major. The mostly ceremonial pistol he wore on his field belt stayed in his holster as he walked toward the newly man-made clearing in the jungle.

Being from Calcutta, the UN observer was oblivious to the buzzing of the flies, nor did he detect the stench of death over the normal smells of jungle decay. He was so focused on the tree stumps that he did not see any of the bodies until he stumbled over the one the panther had been feeding on.

The chunks of flesh torn off by the cat had not completely eradicated the bullet wounds. One round had hit the man in the temple. Half of his brain had been expelled from the large exit wound on the other side of his head. Glossy, fat flies swarmed over the exposed brain, laying their eggs in the bloody gray crevices.

The UN observer suddenly backed away from the corpse. A sharp spasm shook him, and he fell to his knees. The acrid stench of his vomit masked the sweet metallic smell of death in the air. Only after his spasms had stopped and he had wiped the sour slime from his mouth did he finally draw his pistol.

THE MURDER of the UN Green Police team created an uproar. An even greater uproar resulted from the illegal logging site that had been discovered along with the bodies. The preservation of the Amazon rain forests was one of the world's major ecological concerns. With the clear-cutting of the last of the Philippine and Malaysian forests, the only old-growth rain forests on the planet were in the Amazon jungles.

The loudest voices raised against Brazil were those of the TASA nations, the Triple Alliance of South America, which included Argentina, Peru and Bolivia. They were outraged at the environmental crime and threatened to invade Brazil if the people responsible for it were not severely punished. They also demanded that the Brazilian government step down and a new government be formed, a government that would provide iron-clad guarantees that the rain forest would be protected against such outrages.

The Brazilian government claimed to have no knowledge of either the death of the Green Police unit or the extensive logging activities that had been uncovered. But they were not believed. After all, if the UN had been forced to step in to protect the Amazon from further environmental damage, how could they not have known about the logging? In fact, it was widely believed that the Brazilian government itself had been behind the destruction of the rain forest.

The Brazilians flatly refused the excessive TASA demands and, when the TASA nations threatened to invade if they did not accede to the demands, they prepared to defend themselves against the TASA forces.

As the leader of TASA, Argentina secretly welcomed Brazil's reaction. Governed by a military council, Spanish-speaking Argentina was South America's fastest growing high-tech industrial power and welcomed any excuse to extend its dominance over the region. Its arms industry was particularly well advanced, specializing in the manufacture of powered fighting suits, AFVs, missiles and infantry small arms. The country also had a space program that had launched South America's first space station.

The thing that Argentina did not have, however, was room for a rapidly expanding population brought on by a prosperous economy. Population-control programs sponsored by the UN were not popular in that part of the world. Uruguay and Paraguay had already been absorbed by Argentina in 2026, adding a half million square kilometers to Argentinean territory. The long-standing Falkland Islands dispute had also been settled when England ceded the islands back to Argentina rather than go to war again. But even with these territorial gains, Argentina needed more room for its rapidly expanding population and saw Portuguese-speaking Brazil as the place to get it.

Bolivia and Peru, the junior partners in TASA, were not as well-off as Argentina, but they shared her dreams of dominating the region. With the eradication of the last coca tree in 2018, however, their economies were almost completely agriculturally based, and they could do little to advance the TASA goals beyond providing a market for Argentinean goods and manpower.

In an attempt to exploit the great untapped resources in the Andes Mountains, Peru and Bolivia had invited the Han Chinese to advise and assist them in developing new resource-based industries. China's resources were quickly becoming exhausted, and she desperately needed the raw materials, as well as a place for her excess population.

Since Brazil was under United Nations supervision, the UN denounced the Argentinean military buildup and stationed troops along the Brazilian borders with the TASA nations in an attempt to keep the peace. The Argentineans countered by stating that since even the UN Green Police were so obviously unable to protect the rain forest, they had no choice but to invade Brazil to ensure its safety.

While the issue was being talked to death in the chambers of the UN, the United States Expeditionary Force—USEF—went on alert for deployment to South America. Prestocked supplies were gone over, aircraft and skimmers were maintained, weapons were double-checked, tactical plans were made and up-to-date information was gathered about the strength and deployment of the TASA forces moving against Brazil. Most of all, however, individual training was increased.

The TASA military was a modern armed force. For the most part, their weapons and equipment were second only to those of the Peacekeepers. Once more the Peacekeepers would be going up against superior forces. But this time the hostiles would also be well armed, and the only way to even those odds was with superior training.

The world had come to rely on the Peacekeepers, who were formed in 2006 after the short-lived Arab-Israeli nuclear exchange of 2004. Military strike forces had eliminated nuclear weapons worldwide, but a regular globally effective force was clearly needed to nip future military expansionism in the bud.

The United States and Russia had responded to the call, and the soldiers of these elite groups were the best that talent, training and high-tech equipment could ever advance onto the battlefields of the world. The Peacekeepers drew their swords and marked the line on the sand in front of them. An aggressor crossed that line at his peril.

2

Fort Benning, Georgia—9 November

United States Expeditionary Force Staff Sergeant Kat Wallenska led her recon team through the steaming tropical jungle. Strung out in a line formation, they were moving along a sluggish, water-lily-choked stream, searching for a hostile unit that had been reported in the area. Towering trees blocked the noonday sun, and vines and dense undergrowth impeded the progress of the five grunts through the ankle-deep mud but they pressed on.

Wallenska's team this time was not the veteran Strider Alpha recon team she usually led in combat. This was a team made up of USEF recon trainees, men and women who hoped someday to wear the coveted rifle green Peacekeeper beret with the black-and-gold recon flash.

Not only was the recon team made up for this exercise, but the dense jungle they were moving through was also made up. This particular piece of terrain existed only in the computer-generated image known as virtual reality or cyberspace. The computer-generated simulation included not only the sights and sounds of the jungle, but the smells, as well. The virtual reality of the Peacekeeper cyberspace training module, the cyber tank, was the best that twenty-first-century technology could create.

The computer could have as easily put the trainees in the Sahara sand dunes under a blistering sun, the North Pole in the dead of the long polar winter or in the middle of Mexico City during the annual spring riots. Any place on earth was as close as the sprawling Fort Benning cyber tank. A select few Peacekeepers had even undergone space-suit combat training under the one-sixth normal gravity of the moon's surface. That had been more difficult to simulate because of the harnesses needed to reduce their weight, but anywhere on Earth was a snap.

The recon grunts were wearing the special cyberspace training helmets and suits for this exercise that relayed the computer-generated image to their sight and senses. The suits also transmitted every movement of the team members back to the computer so it could incorporate them into the virtual reality it was generating.

Though the cyber helmets blocked normal vision, when the recon team pointman dropped down and signaled for a halt, the computer sent an image of him to each of the other team members. But they did not see him wearing the slick gray cyber training suit with the full helmet and carrying a training rifle. They saw him in mud-splattered USEF chameleon cammos, full assault harness and helmet, carrying a 5 mm M-25 LAR, or light assault rifle.

To an outside observer watching the team go through the exercise, it was like watching a weird, slow-motion dance being performed in a huge empty room. In fact, except for the cyberspace team working in their control booth, there was absolutely nothing in the room except for the five figures crouched down in the middle of the open floor.

To the team's pointman, trainee Bill Harris, however, he was in a shadowy jungle of huge trees blocking the sun, vines, dense undergrowth and sticky black mud. Other than the whine of unseen insects, he heard nothing but the sound of his own labored breathing. When he also saw nothing, he stood and waved the rest of the team forward again.

He hadn't even taken his first step when a hostile broke from cover in the underbrush not five meters to his right front. The automatic shotgun in the man's hands blazed fire, and Harris froze in place. When the grunt didn't react instantly, the computer shifted the hostile's aim and Harris took a blast of 12-gauge buckshot in the belly.

The image the cyber helmet showed his eyes included the muzzle-blast of the shotgun, as well as the feral snarl on the face of the hostile firing at him. The cyber suit delivered a blow to his lower belly as if he had taken a hit from the blast of buckshot.

"Medic!" he screamed. "Get a medic! I'm hit!"

Harris dropped to the floor of the training module and curled up into a ball, his hands pressed tightly to his belly. His breath came in gasps, and his med readouts were going crazy. He was dying.

Flipping up her cyberspace helmet visor, Kat Wallenska ran to him, knelt by his side and pried his hands away from his belly. Raising his cyber helmet visor, she forced his head down so his eyes could see the cyberspace training suit he wore.

The metallic gray sheen of the material over his abdomen was unbroken. There was no jagged, gaping wound in his belly, no bluish, slick intestines bulging out, no blood spurting from his aorta. His eyes, however, couldn't see what Kat saw. His brain was locked into the virtual reality of cyberspace, and his eyes told him that he was dying.

Cyberspace training had its definite advantages. No matter what the terrain, the cyberspace computer faithfully generated the sensations—heat or cold, sun or shade, vegetation or sand—that went with that part of the world. It also supplied the hostile forces, as well as the supporting fire and vehicles of the friendlies. In fact, it supplied everything that went with real combat except the fear and fatigue. The trainee's mind supplied that.

But there were those who got lost and couldn't differentiate between virtual and actual reality—cyber freaks they were called. They were the ultimate addicts, men and women who chose not to experience life, but to duck into the deepest recesses of their own minds and live their fantasies instead. All it took was a cyberspace computer, a cyber suit and some basic programming skills. It helped to have one of the bootleg starter kits, sex, violence, drugs or whatever was your interest. But even without a starter program, it was easy enough to roll your own hit, as they said.

Few cyber freaks ever made it into the Peacekeepers. They were screened out in the psychological evaluation every trainee went through, but it looked as if this one had slipped through the psych screen.

Drawing back her hand, Kat slapped Harris full in the face, snapping his head to the side with the blow. "Wake up, dickhead!" she screamed. "It's a fucking cyber dream, Harris! You're okay! You're in the cyber tank and you're not going to die!"

Harris's eyes rolled back in their sockets, and he gurgled as if his lungs were filling with blood.

The medic shoved Kat aside and knelt beside the trainee. He was raising the autoinjector to give him a dose of a sedative when his med readouts went flatline. He switched the injector to adrenaline and went for a heart shot.

When CPR and adrenaline didn't restore Harris's heart function, the medic looked up from the body. "What happened here, Wallenska?"

"He fucking freak locked." The disgust was clear in her voice. "When he took a cyber shot in the guts, he completely freaked out."

"Well—" the medic shook his head "—he sure as hell isn't cyber dead. He's dead for real."

MAJOR ALEXANDER F. Rosemont, the Echo Company commander, was in the force ops center doing a holotank recon of southern Brazil when his comlink beeped with a message about Harris's death. "Shit!" he muttered.

Rosemont was blond and blue eyed like his namesake, Alexander the Great, but that was where the similarity ended. The legendary Macedonian king had been a small wiry man, and Rosemont was tall, muscular and in top physical condition. Just topping six feet tall, Rosemont would have been considered a giant in the age of Alexander. As it was, though, he looked no different than any other thirty-two-year-old professional soldier in the USEF.

LTC Taylor Michaels, the force operations officer, looked up from the holotank. This was one USEF staff officer who did not look like a misplaced academic. The authoritative way he wore his uniform with the combat infantry badge, jump wings and recon shoulder flash showed that he had been on the sharp end of the stick more than once. His dark black skin, shaved head and dead cigar clamped between his teeth only added to his kick-ass image. Down in the line companies, Michaels was known as "Mad Mike."

"What's the problem?" he asked around the stub of the dead cigar.

"I just lost a recon trainee in the cyber tank, sir. He freak locked and died."

Michaels didn't even pretend to have sympathy for the dead trainee. As far as he was concerned, cyber freaks were the scum of the earth. Playing in the cyber tanks was fun, but anyone who got locked onto the computer fantasies was brain burned and better off dead.

"Good fucking riddance," Michaels growled. "I don't know why the psych screen can't pick out those fucking freaks and eliminate their asses before we waste good training time on them."

"I couldn't agree more, sir, but Harris's death still leaves me shorthanded in the recon platoon. Even if that entire bunch of trainees had finished the cycle, I'd have still been four people short."

"You're just going to have to go with what you have," Michaels stated flatly. "We don't have time to run anyone else through the program."

The Peacekeepers had been on a Dep Three alert for the past week now. From all indications, the situation in Brazil was going to go ballistic at any moment. The TASA–United Nations standoff was going the way of all UN negotiations, nowhere. Once again the UN was failing miserably, and by the time the Peacekeepers were sent in, it would be too late for anything but the solutions that could only be found on the battlefield.

The force commander had argued for a preemptive strike at the TASA military buildup in Argentina, but had been turned down flat. Even so, they wouldn't get the call to battle until it was too late and the TASA forces had launched their invasion of Brazil.

Once more the Peacekeepers would go in and spend their lives to correct a situation that should have never gotten out of hand in the first place. Before this was over, more names would be chiseled on the black granite wall in the USEF headquarters, names of the men and women who had given their lives so that politicians could protect their miserable asses.

It was a stupid way to run the world. But as long as there were politicians who only talked about peace and were not prepared to back up their empty words with positive action to keep the peace, there would be war. In the year 2030, where there was war, you would find the USEF. And where you found the Peacekeepers, you found Echo Company's recon platoon leading the way. Shorthanded or not, Echo Company was always the first in and the last out. That was their job, and it was their pride to always do their job.

Rosemont took a deep breath. "Yes, sir."

THE ECHO COMPANY briefing room was crowded by the time Rosemont got back to his unit. He paused for a moment in the open door to look over the faces of his officers and key senior NCOs waiting for him.

The recon platoon leader, First Lieutenant Ashley Wells, was in animated conversation with his XO, First Lieutenant Thomas "Mick" Sullivan. As usual, Ashley was dominating the conversation by force of her blond beauty and her choice of the more pungent words of the English language.

Ashley was known to the Peacekeepers as "Ash-and-Trash." Her nickname came not only for her effective use of English, but also for what she left behind at the end of an operation. When Ashley Wells's troops were done with an area, all that was left was ash and trash.

Mick was trying to hold his own in the conversation, but as usual, Ashley was verbally beating up on him. Of all the Echo Company officers, he and Ash had worked together the longest, so he was used to it.

Second Platoon leader First Lieutenant Jubal Early Butler Stuart and First Lieutenant Hank Rivera of the weapons platoon both looked bored as they waited for the briefing. Jeb would quickly become unbored as soon as he got out in the field, however.

Although his first three names were different from the famous Confederate cavalry officer with the same initials and last name, everyone thought he had been named after General Jeb Stuart. Being a son of the Old South, however, he didn't mind at all. In fact, his first two names, Jubal Early, were those of another, less distinguished Confederate general his family claimed descent from. The Butler part was from his mother's family and had nothing to do with the American Civil War, or "The War between the States," as most Southerners still preferred to call it.

Jeb was happiest when he was reenacting an exploit of his non-namesake, a raid deep into enemy territory. The difference was that he and his Second Platoon raced for the objective in Tilt Wings, not mounted on horseback. Which was a good thing, as this Jeb Stuart had never ridden a horse.

Rivera was a typical cannon cocker. He only came alive when his rocket mortars were hammering some poor bastard to bits. The rest of the time, he was content to enjoy the good life. Rosemont didn't mind his laid-back attitude because he knew that when it came to crunch time Rivera's guns would be there—on time and on target.

The conversations stopped when Rosemont marched up to the front of the room and stepped behind the podium. "Before I get started here," he said, "I have a couple of announcements to make. First off, Lieutenant Wells, Lieutenant Sullivan, front and center."

The two officers got up from their seats with frowns on their faces, walked to the front of the room and stood at attention facing their company commander.

"I want everyone to notice," Rosemont said, "that these two officers are out of uniform."

Ash and Mick exchanged blank looks. What in the hell was Rosemont talking about? The duty uniform for a Dep Three was chameleon camouflage battle dress with the green beret, and that's what they were wearing.

"I will not tolerate seeing my officers out of uniform." Rosemont grinned as he took a hard copy from his pocket and gave it away. "Particularly my captains.

"Attention to orders," Rosemont announced. "Headquarters United States Expeditionary Force Orders 2281-30, dated 9 November 2030. The following personnel are hereby promoted to temporary rank of captain as of this date. First Lieutenant Wells, Ashley T., First Lieutenant Sullivan, Thomas M., Signed, Bernard T. Jacobson, Colonel commanding."

Rosemont stepped up to Mick and handed him a pair of captain's bars. "Congratulations, Mick."

Sullivan grinned from ear to ear. "Thank you, sir."

"Congratulations, Ash."

"You bastard." She leaned forward and whispered, "You could have warned me about this last night."

"I kinda forgot," he said, smiling wolfishly. "Someone kept distracting me."

Ash grinned. "Asshole."

"Now that the formalities are over—" Rosemont switched on the holomap at the end of the room "—let's get to the briefing. Here's what we're going to do when we finally get the word to go down there and do it."

There was a buzz in the room as a map of the Brazilian-Argentinean border region appeared. "Our primary drop zone is here." He pointed out a lightly wooded area to the west of a valley. "We will lead the drop and secure the area for the other companies. After we're down, the Hulks will drop into the mouth of the valley. Charlie and Delta companies will . . ."

He quickly laid out the initial troop dispositions and unit responsibilities. He didn't bother going into long-term tactical plans, because that would depend on the TASA reaction to finding the Peacekeepers in their path and there was no telling what they would do. That was why the entire force was making this drop.

When he was finished, he switched off the holomap. "Any questions?" he asked as his eyes scanned the room.

"If not, pick up your mission packets on the way out. The Old Man expects it to go ballistic within the next twenty-four hours, so brief your people and stay frosty."

3

Fort Benning—9 November

Rosemont intercepted Ashley before she left the briefing room. "How do those new tracks feel, Captain Wells?"

For well over a hundred years, the twin silver bars denoting an Army captain's rank had been known as railroad tracks from the old days when trains had run on two rails. What few trains there were in the twenty-first century rode on magnetic monorails, but the name had held.

Ashley smiled. "They feel fine, Major. And it's about fucking time they showed up."

Rosemont laughed. "I thought you'd say something like that." He reached out and touched her shoulder. "I've got to get back to it, see you later tonight."

"Don't be too late," she said.

He grinned widely. "I'll try not to be."

ROSEMONT AND ASHLEY were both bone weary when they finally got to their quarters later that night. They were not too tired, though, to make love before they went to sleep. Now that they had finally decided to become lovers, they wasted no opportunity to be together.

To live together in garrison, as well as on the battlefield, had not been an easy decision for either of them to make, but for totally different reasons. For Ashley, making a lover's commitment had carried a fear of losing her cherished independence.

Most of the mystery about the fiercely independent Ashley Wells was about why she had joined the Peacekeepers in the first place. Since she had been a small child, she had never willingly submitted herself to authority of any kind. As one of the many daughters of the UniCard magnate Winston W. Wells, she had been born to unlimited wealth. With that kind of money behind her, she could get away with doing things her way, even in her own family. In fact, the reason she had gotten into her only previous sexual relationship had been that her father had so strongly disapproved of the man.

Her college career had been checkered because she was constantly in conflict with the authorities over campus rules. Had it not been for her famous last name, she probably would not have graduated. With the exception of the tight rein she kept on her sexuality and the fact that she never took drugs or allowed herself to get drunk, she almost went out of her way to break the rules and resented authority in any form.

Why she had chosen one of the most disciplined professions in the world and had willingly subjected herself to the rigors of military discipline, no one knew. Least of all USEF Captain Ashley Wells. And now she had submitted to the most rigorous discipline of all, that of falling in love. No one had been more surprised that she had done this than the man whose bed she was now sharing.

For Rosemont, however, his fears of making the commitment revolved around the fact that he would have to order the woman he loved into combat to fight and maybe die.

When he'd been in the Regular Army, he'd had girlfriends when he'd been stationed in the States, but never for very long. Even though the RA lived a more settled life than the Peacekeepers, he'd always been on the move. If it wasn't a change of duty station as he'd worked his way up through the ranks, it was training maneuvers that had taken him away for months at a time. Women who wanted to live the life of an Army camp follower were a dying breed, and he'd not been fortunate enough to meet one of them.

For years he'd thought that it would be a long time, if ever, before he would be able to live like other men and have a wife or permanent lover. Back then he'd never even dreamed that he'd find his mate wearing a uniform. Then he'd been accepted into the Peacekeepers and met Ashley Wells.

Like every man who had ever met her, he'd been immediately taken by her stunning beauty. Her golden blond hair, gray eyes, perfect features and aristocratic bearing were the stuff of erotic dreams. Women who looked like Ashley Wells were not found in anyone's army that he'd ever seen. More attractive than her beauty, though, was her fiery temperament, which was so different from his more even-paced view of the world.

Very early on in his military career, Rosemont had learned to keep his temper and his emotions under tight control. It wasn't that he didn't feel strongly about things, because he did. He could also lose his temper when anger was required, and when he did, his officers and NCOs had learned to stay out of his way. It was just that he had come to understand that he was a better commander when he kept himself under control.

Ashley, however, wore her emotions like a banner, and there was never a doubt about what she thought. And if there was, she'd be glad to tell you to your face. Right in your face, as a matter of fact, as she had done to him several times when he first took command of the company. Initially she had been rebellious to the point of insubordination, and he had even seriously considered asking the colonel to transfer her out of the unit.

He had seen her value to the company as the recon platoon leader, however, and had put off requesting her transfer. Also he quickly came to realize that even though she could be a pain in the ass, her explosive emotional vitality appealed to him. He always felt more alive when he was around her, and the longer he had been around her, the more he had wanted to be with her all the time.

As her company commander, there had been several more times that he had regretted not having gotten rid of her when he'd had the chance. But all that was in the past. Now he didn't want to think of not having her a part of his daily life. The problem was that now she was living with him, and he had to face the possibility that he would be responsible for her death.

Right after they had started sharing their BOQ suite, he had briefly considered requesting transfer to a staff position so he wouldn't be the one who had to order her into battle. Even if he did that, she would still be at risk, and Ash-and-Trash would have resigned rather than take a noncombat staff job. The only thing that would change was that someone else would be giving her the orders instead of him. Since he didn't trust anyone to make better combat decisions than he did, he'd quickly dropped that idea.

"Alex?" she murmured softly.

Jolted out of his thoughts, he felt a bemused smile tug at his mouth. Damn women, why did they always want to talk afterward? "Hmm?"

"Wake up!"

"I'm awake, I'm awake." He rolled over to face her, his hands automatically going to their favorite places.

"Goddammit! Knock that off," she snapped, pulling away.

Now he was completely awake. "Okay, what's wrong?"

"Alex...?"

"Yes."

She snuggled over against him and laid her head against his chest. "If something goes wrong..." she started hesitantly, "I want you to know that I've listed you as my official next of kin."

"What do you mean?"

"My accounts. You know, the stocks, trusts and the rest of that bullshit, I signed them all over to you in case I get zeroed."

"Jesus, Ash, you didn't have to do that. We aren't married or anything like that."

She continued as if she had not heard him. "And if I do buy the farm, I want you to promise me one thing."

"What's that?"

"I want you to take the money and get the hell out of this business. Go somewhere, find yourself another woman and live your life out in peace. You'll have more than enough money to live three lifetimes without lifting a finger."

The thought of her getting killed chilled him in a way he couldn't deal with at all. "You're not going to get killed, Ash. You're too tough to kill. And," he added, "far too battle smart."

"Promise me, please."

He heard the tears in her voice. "I promise I'll quit. Love, I promise."

"If you don't, I swear to Christ I'll come back and haunt your sorry ass."

He laughed and held her tightly to him.

AN HOUR BEFORE DAWN the next morning, TASA's mechanized forces struck across the Brazilian border. Led by Argentinean heavy infantry in Toro fighting suits, an armored spearhead brushed past the thin line of UN observers and thrust deep into southern Brazil.

The Brazilian forces valiantly tried to stem the TASA advance, throwing their light tanks and armored skimmers against the powered fighting suits and heavy armor. The Brazilians were not cowards, and they fought bravely. However, not only were they badly outnumbered, but they were also badly outgunned. Slowly they were forced to fall back in the face of the onslaught.

In the UN, tempers exploded with the predawn report of the invasion. The Brazilian ambassador had to be forcefully removed from the chambers when he attacked the Argentinean delegate and tried his best to strangle him on CNN international holovee.

Rubbing his bruised throat, the delegate took the rostrum and defended his nation's action. He argued that since the UN observers were obviously impotent—"castrated eunuchs" was what he actually called them in Spanish—someone had to defend the threatened rain forests.

CNN accurately translated the envoy's remarks, which only added to the controversy.

In the United States Senate, the FemiParty senator from the state of Oregon got up and, responding to the accuracy of the CNN translation, launched into one of her tirades about the sexist filth that was being beamed to the children in American homes. She concluded with a demand that the United States withdraw from the United Nations immediately. The Democratic senator from California took the rostrum next and delivered an impassioned speech about the rights of transsexuals to serve in the armed forces. It was two hours before the Senate was able to get back to the matter at hand, the invasion of Brazil.

By midmorning of the first day, the Brazilians had lost over a hundred kilometers of their territory to the fast-moving TASA columns and they were still driving hard for the city of Curitiba. Once it was in their hands, it would serve as a base for a continued assault on the capital city, Brasilia.

Even though the situation was critical, the UN was having even less success dealing with the emergency than the Brazilian army. As always, the Security Council was divided along lines that had nothing to do with the issue in front of them.

Most of the South American nations thought that an Argentinean victory would be good for business. Europe and the United States saw the invasion as a dangerous precedent that had to be crushed. The Arabic states sided with Argentina because she had promised them oil-drilling concessions in their untapped Atlantic oil fields. The Greens in several nations combined their influence to support the TASA military action. They felt that it was regrettable but necessary to kill Brazilians to protect the rain forest.

It was finally decided to try to contain the TASA advance rather than take more positive steps to end the war. Since the Argentinean forces were all ground units with only supporting tactical aircraft, not strategic, the effort would be made on the ground only.

No missile strikes or bombers would be brought into play to do the job.

Once more the American Peacekeepers would be sent to fight and die on the ground of a foreign land.

WHILE THIS DECISION was being made, the Peace-keepers were on the tarmac at Lawson Airfield waiting for the word to board their C-36B Valkyrie supersonic assault transports. Their gear had already been loaded along with the ammunition and supplies to sustain three days' combat. All they needed was the word to go.

Sergeant John Ironstone, Kat Wallenska's assistant team leader, lay stretched out on his back letting the thin winter Georgia sun bathe his dark copper-colored face and blue-black hair. A Comanche from a large ranch outside of Oklahoma City, Ironstone considered himself to be a modern Indian warrior following a long, proud tradition. He didn't ride a horse to war anymore, but the skimmers and Tilt Wings carried him to battle far faster than any horse could have.

He did, however, follow the Comanche tradition of wearing war paint on his face. Three broad, black stripes adorned each of his cheeks, slanting upward. No one could see the war paint when his helmet visor was down, but he knew it was there and that was what mattered. The paint was his honor and strength, and he would no more have considered going into battle without it than he would leaving his light assault rifle behind.

As he relaxed, his eyes followed Kat Wallenska as she paced back and forth on the tarmac. Her helmet was under her arm, and the weak sun glinted off the silver skull earring in her right ear. Usually the tough Polish American recon sergeant was the picture of calm, as frosty as deep space. Today, though, she was doing a good imitation of a newbie waiting for her first drop.

"Yo, Kat!" he called out.

"What ya want, Ironman?"

"Why don't you sit down, woman, we might be here all day. Get frosty, you're making me nervous marching back and forth that way."

"Screw you, Ironman, and the horse you rode in on."

He grinned. "Kat, Kat. Is that any way to talk to your favorite redskin?"

"Don't give me any of your shit today, Ironstone. I mean it. I'm not in the mood for it."

"What's wrong, Katrina?"

Kat dropped to a crouch beside him. "Jesus, why don't they just send us on our way and get it over with?"

The Indian grinned broadly. "You know that's not how it works, Kat. They can't send us until the situation has gone completely to shit. If they send us in too soon, we'll get it all wrapped up before they've even finished running off their mouths and posing for the holovee cameras."

"Dickheads," she snarled. "We're supposed to stop shit like this from happening."

"Shut up and soldier, Wallenska."

Kat laughed. "Fuck you, Ironman."

A few paces away, on the lowered rear ramp of one of the Valkyries, Mick Sullivan was watching a movie on the small portable holoplayer he always carried wherever he went. An otherwise rational man, Sullivan was seriously obsessed with old movies. His specialty was old war movies, and at the drop of a hat, he could deliver an hour-long lecture on any topic from the classic John Wayne Indian war–cavalry movies to Rambo as a symbol of urban social unrest in late-twentieth-century American urban society.

Sullivan was popular with the grunts because he could always be counted on to use his entire personal weight allowance to pack his little holoplayer and as many laser disks as possible. The fact that all of his disks were of movies made before the turn of the century didn't bother the troops too much. They'd watch anything to break the boredom of waiting to go to war.

Rosemont walked over to the impromptu movie theater to see what Sullivan was watching this morning. He couldn't think of any movies that had ever been made of South American wars other than drug raids. It would be interesting to see what Mick had chosen to inspire him today.

To his complete amazement, Sullivan was showing the classic *Patton.* Dressed in World War II German uniforms, the Spanish army was attacking across what was supposed to be the Tunisian desert toward George C. Scott's dug-in U.S. troops. The infantry was accompanied by hundreds of American-made Spanish tanks painted gray with German crosses.

Suddenly the desert exploded as the artillery began to fall on the attackers. The American tanks broke out of cover and added their fire to the maelstrom. The camera shifted to Patton, who said, "Rommel, you magnificent bastard. I read your book."

Rosemont didn't know of any book that would explain what was going on down in Brazil or how best to deal with it. If there was, he sure as hell would have read it himself.

As the Germans retreated across the desert, Rosemont walked back across the tarmac to his waiting plane.

4

Over the South Atlantic—10 November

Alex Rosemont could smell himself and he didn't like what he smelled. The acrid reek of his adrenaline-laden sweat cut through the normal stale odors of tightly packed humanity in the C-36B Valkyrie super-sonic assault transport. And the closer they got to the drop zone, the ranker he smelled.

Looking down to the other end of the row of half-opened recon drop capsules on the opposite side of the plane, he spotted Ashley's short-cropped blond hair. She was sitting with her helmet in her lap and her head laid back against the seat webbing, sleeping as peace-fully as if she were in their bed back at Fort Benning. Seeing her so comfortable under these circumstances pissed him off to no end.

She was the only person who knew that he had an almost paralyzing fear of heights and hated capsule jumping more than anything else in the world. When he'd finally told her about his phobia, she had tried to understand and had been as sympathetic about it as she could. But the least she could do now to show him that she understood was to stay awake while he was suffering.

He had been able to successfully hide this particular fear of his throughout his military career, even when he had gone through jump school, and he was sure as hell not going to let his control slip now. Any man was allowed to refuse to make a drop whenever he wanted, but he would have to turn in his green beret and jump wings as soon as the plane landed.

Rosemont had wanted to join the Peacekeepers almost from the moment he had been commissioned in the Regular Army infantry, but it was not that easy to get a slot in the elite force. Of every one hundred men, enlisted or commissioned, who applied to join the USEF, only three were chosen to don the proud green beret. He had worked hard to get his beret and he was not about to give it up. He would make this capsule jump even if it killed him. Which, of course, was exactly what he was afraid of.

He heard the electric whine of the plane's wing sweep motors and felt the Valkyrie assault transport suddenly decelerate and go subsonic. Lowering his helmet visor, he flicked on his helmet nav display and saw that they were approaching the drop zone, a grassy wooded valley to the southwest of Passo Fundo in southern Brazil. Once on the ground, they would be in a blocking position along the main avenue of advance for the TASA armored forces slashing deep into Brazilian territory.

The Peacekeepers' tactical plan was simple: stop the TASA spearhead before it could reach São Paulo, cut it off from its supporting elements and then destroy it piecemeal. To effect that end, the light infantry companies had to secure the flanks of the battle zone while the heavy infantry went head-to-head with the Argentinean powered fighting suits.

Echo Company had been given the western flank in the woods bordering the valley while Delta and Charlie companies were to hold the plains to the east. The Alpha and Bravo heavies would drop in at the mouth of the valley with their backs to the river at the north.

As always, though, the recon platoons of the light infantry companies were going in first to secure the DZs and prepare the way for the heavies. That meant a fast recon drop, the worst kind. Rosemont had the option to come down later with the company headquarters element, a nice low drop in standard infantry capsules. But he always had to be with the point elements of his company because it gave him a better view of what was going on, and today that meant a recon drop. He felt the cold sweat break out again and would have killed for a shower.

When his earphone bonged with the suit-up signal, Rosemont closed the jump capsule shell around his chest and dogged it down tight. Locking his helmet visor, he checked the helmet seals and turned on the oxygen supply for the trip down.

After making a quick function check on the drop capsule, he stood up at the end of the jump line and shuffled forward to the capsule launchers on the sides of the aircraft. His helmet visor display still showed everything in the green as he stepped back into the launch chamber. He felt the clamps secure him and the magnoelastic joints of his capsule stiffen to lock his legs together and hold his arms tightly to his sides for the drop.

He knew some lunatics who still jumped out of airplanes with nothing more than a thin nylon parachute strapped to their backs. Making the drop in a capsule was bad enough. The mere thought of stepping out into empty space without a jump capsule was enough to make him want to puke.

He was on the end of the stick and had to wait until the rest of the recon platoon had been launched before he felt the slam of the ejection against his shoulders. As always, his stomach lurched and he clamped his jaws together, sucking in the stale, dry oxygen as deeply as he could. As his capsule cleared the launcher, it bounced in the turbulent airstream before the stabilizers snapped out and caught the air.

Once the ride smoothed out, Rosemont flicked on the drop display on his visor and watched the altimeter swiftly count down. His speed was within the limits for a recon capsule, but dangerously on the high side. He rested his right index finger on the trigger for the speed brakes, but didn't pop a retard. Right now the recon drop capsules were as stealthy as was technologically possible. Even if the Argies were right under him, they'd never see him. His radar signature was less than that of a small sparrow. But the instant that he hit the retards, he would show up as if he were riding in a lead-lined hot-air balloon. His screen showed that none of the other capsules had deployed their retards, and if they could do it, so could he.

As the altimeter numbers ticked off like an over-revved clock, he watched the other capsules on his screen. They were approaching the deploy point at well over three hundred miles per hour, but no one had popped their capsule's canopy yet. They were riding them all the way down as if they were bombing the drop zone.

He felt his testicles suck up into his belly when he thought of hitting the ground at that speed. The capsule had a reserve chute if the main failed, but it was useless below a certain height. Hell, even the main chute was useless unless you deployed it in time.

When he saw the first capsule pop its chute, he instinctively triggered his own. The opening shock slammed him against the capsule webbing, but it was over in an instant as the canopy fully deployed. He had opened low and, falling as fast as they had been, he was still approaching the ground too damn fast. He reached for the "chicken switch" to the emergency retro rocket, but was too late. He hit the ground hard, knocking the breath out of him.

Recon platoon was already deploying in the woods by the time he got out of his capsule. "Have a nice trip down, Bold Lancer?" Ashley spoke over his comlink, the amusement plain in her voice.

"Just fine, Bold Strider," he replied, steadying his voice. "Status?"

"We're all down and deploying. No sign of hostile activity yet."

That went along with the last satellite Intel update
he had received before the drop, but the TASA forces
were moving so fast that they couldn't depend on
hour-old Intel. "Affirm. Secure the DZ and send the
all clear."

"It's been sent."

"Affirm. Get your teams out."

"They're on their way."

Ashley's five recon teams were deploying in an arc
facing south to protect the drop zone. It would be a
while before the Bat unmanned aerial vehicles would
be sent up to give him long-range battlefield surveil-
lance. Until then he had to work with the satellite
feeds. Given the thick ground cover of the local terrain, he wanted to get his recon teams out there so they
could send him their bare eyeball and battlefield sensor input. This was no time for surprises.

While the recon teams took up their positions, Sullivan's First Platoon grunts started their drop. They
were quickly followed by Stuart's Second Platoon and
Rivera's weapons platoon. For the next half an hour,
the predawn sky was filled with drop capsules.

Once everyone was down, the grunts started digging in. Usually, the light infantry platoons stayed
loose and didn't fortify their positions. Their instant
mobility was usually their best defense. On this occa-
sion, though, they were facing a force as well armed
and as mobile as their own, and the effort spent digging in might well pay off.

Though Echo Company was designated a light infantry unit, it could stand up to a standard infantry

battalion and beat them into the ground. The Peace-keeper heavy infantry companies could take on a full regiment and wipe them off the face of the earth. The USEF was small but powerful. Man for man, or woman for woman, for that matter, they were the best troops in the world.

Much of their battlefield superiority could be credited to their superior weapons and equipment. With very few exceptions, the Peacekeepers had the absolute best that twenty-first-century technology could produce. The problem this time was that they weren't going up against a second- or third-rate army where their technological superiority was automatically going to give them the edge over sheer numbers.

The TASA forces, particularly the Argentinean contingent, were well armed with some of the most modern weaponry available anywhere. For the most part, the Argentinean arms industry was as high-tech as any in the world. Along with being well armed, the TASA military combine was the largest armed force in South America. From the Intel that USEF had received, a full Argentinean division was deployed in the attack on Brazil and two more were standing by in reserve.

The Peacekeepers' tactical plan was simple and straightforward and should work as planned. Still, as Rosemont knew all too well, no plan, no matter how well thought out, ever survived the initial contact with the enemy. Particularly not an enemy as large and as well armed as this one.

Now that the Peacekeepers were down and deployed, all they could do was wait. The data flashing in over the taclink indicated that they would not have to wait very long. The TASA point elements were racing toward them as fast as they could.

THE ADVANCING ARGIES were pushing hard. Under a protective umbrella of Tac Air fighters and gunships, an armored skimmer column was running flat out up the valley toward the Uruguay River to secure a crossing point. Now that the Brazilian army was in full retreat, the Argies were exploiting their collapse. The skimmers were well out in front, leaving the slower TASA heavy armor and fighting-suit infantry units to bring up the rear.

When the hostile skimmers first appeared, there were over a dozen of the armored vehicles running in an extended column formation. After they reached the middle of the valley, they fanned out into the pampas grass and scrub brush, their light green-and-tan camouflage paint making them blend in with the terrain. Their camouflage, however, did not prevent the Peacekeepers from targeting them.

To further mask their positions, the Peacekeepers had not activated either their jamming devices or their active sensors yet. So far, all they were using were their optical and passive targeting devices. They would serve well enough for the opening salvos of the ambush.

The Peacekeepers let the Argie skimmers come in close, five hundred meters, before taking them under fire. The lead skimmer went up in a ball of flame when a Pit Bull ground-assault missile punched through its front plate and set off its fuel tanks. The fireball was still forming above the stricken vehicle when the second, third and fourth skimmers were hit. The headlong TASA assault was stopped cold in its tracks.

The rest of the skimmers frantically tried to get out of the kill zone, but the Charlie and Delta company missile gunners had them zeroed. Round after round scored direct hits on the speeding vehicles. The last one was taken out with a hit on its left rear quarter as it was retreating. This time, though, the crew escaped before the vehicle took a second hit and exploded.

The Argie Tac Air swooped down to try to even the score and cover the retreat of the skimmers, but fire-support Thunderbolt antiaircraft missile batteries were waiting and ready for them. The Thunderbolt hyperspeed kinetic missiles flashed through the clear blue sky like lightning.

When a Thunderbolt hit a gunship, not only did the missile punch its way completely through it, but its kinetic energy was also instantly transformed into heat. That heat instantly transformed an aircraft into aerial junk, or a fireball, depending on where it hit. The end result, either way, was the same. Within seconds the sky had been completely swept clean of hostile aircraft.

For the next several minutes, the only sounds on the battlefield were the crackling hiss of the fires and the muffled detonations of ammunition cooking off inside the burning vehicles.

THE AMBUSH HAD BEEN successful, but the element of surprise had been lost. It was time to get the full power of the Peacekeeper fighting machine on line, and that meant sending the Bat UAVs up.

Back at the force CP on the other side of the river, the S-2 UAV techs readied their ground-launched versions of the UAV-15C Bat unmanned aerial vehicle for takeoff. Powered by a fully shielded, high-thrust miniature turbine, the three-meter-wide recon flyers carried a full battery of sensors, detectors and jammers in their bellies. With their "mirror skin" covering, which could change color to match the sky they flew through, and the IR shielding on their jet exhaust and their radar jammers, they were almost impossible to detect with anything but the most sophisticated sensors.

The ground-support crew swarmed over two of the Bats, fueling them and checking the data links from the sensors and detectors. As soon as the first flyer was ready, it was hoisted up into the cradle of its zero-length launcher and the jet engine started. Once the exhaust gas temperature was in the green, the UAV controller spooled the small turbine up to full power and punched the button that fired the rocket-assist takeoff unit.

The Bat leaped from its zero-length launcher with a roar and quickly climbed to altitude. The controller held the flyer in a tight orbit over the CP while he ran through a last series of systems checks. When they were completed, he sent the recon bird climbing for altitude over the valley.

A HALF HOUR LATER Rosemont and his officers clustered around the UAV monitor in his jump CP. The monitor was linked to the Bat flying high over the other end of the valley, and the images relayed from the small recon flyer were as good a depiction of the area it was flying over as they would have gotten from a low-level Bubble Top recon flight. Actually it was better. The flyer's multispectrum sensors and detectors could see what the naked eye could not. Specifically they could see through even the most artful camouflage and detect whatever was hiding underneath it.

Right now the Bat was circling at five thousand feet over the far end of the valley. The small recon vehicle's skin was dialed to light-blue, rendering it invisible against the morning sky. The electronic countermeasures jammers in its belly also made it invisible to all spectra of radar detection, including the radars of the TASA antiaircraft missile batteries. Though the missile radars could not see the flyer, to the Bat's sensors, the camouflaged missile launchers couldn't have been any plainer if they'd had laser hologram signs erected over them.

The Bat wasn't focusing on the missile batteries, however; it was watching something far more dangerous. Two battalions of TASA powered fighting-suit heavy infantry were deploying at the southern end of the valley and heading for the Peacekeepers' positions. At their present rate of advance, they would be in the battle zone in less than half an hour.

5

The Passo Fundo Valley—10 November

On his tacscreen, Rosemont watched the Alpha Company Angels and the Bravo Company Bulls move forward out of their positions in the northern end of the valley and deploy southward to meet the hostile heavies. Even with their chameleon camouflage paint, it was not hard to spot them as they moved through the scrub brush and pampas grass. It was difficult to hide a two-meter-tall armored fighting machine that walked like a man.

Every time he saw the Hulks going into battle, Rosemont thanked God once more that he was a light infantry grunt. Even with their heavy armor and devastating firepower, as far as he was concerned, the powered fighting suits were simply too big of a target. There had been those times when he'd wished that he'd had more protection than the thin Kevlar armor inserts in his cammos. Then the thought of having a Hulk wrapped around him had sounded good, real good. But he was not willing to give up the grunt's ability to hide in the weeds or run for it when the shit started flying a little too thick. Even so, he had to admit that the Hulks were very impressive. He just hoped that the Argies were also impressed.

Powered fighting-suit technology was considered to be highly restricted military information in most of the world. The Hulk suits were too potent to allow them to be used by the less stable nations of the world. But, as was always the case with technological secrets, once the genie was out of the bottle, it was difficult to put him back in. This had been the case with nuclear-weapons technology in the last half of the twentieth century and was the case with powered fighting-suit technology in the twenty-first century. Though she was not a world power, Argentina had been able to capture this particular genie and break into this exclusive club.

An American company with good political connections had been able to secure a technology-transfer permit from the U.S. State Department to allow the Argentineans to build powered suits to be used in their logging industry. These were to be simple suits, designed for heavy lifting rather than for speed and agility like the military suits. At the same time, another American company had secured a politically motivated contract to build a ceramal-tile-manufacturing facility for the Argentinean space program.

Powered logging suits armored with ceramal and equipped with the high-tech weapons the Argentineans were famous for equalled heavy infantry powered fighting suits in anyone's language. With the political influence confusing the issue of the technology-transfer permits, no one made the connection until it was too late.

By Peacekeeper standards, the Argentinean Toro suits were somewhat crude. At a height of 2.7 meters and weighing five hundred kilos, they were larger than the Hulk powered suits. Like the bulls they were named for, they were slow and somewhat cumbersome. While not as fast or as agile as the Hulks, they carried better armor and mounted first-rate heavy weapons.

The Toro suits' main gun was a short-barreled 20 mm machine cannon mounted on the right side. A spin-off of the Argentinean space shuttle program involved the adaptation of a remote grappling-arm control system to use with the 20 mm. This allowed the machine cannon to be solidly mounted to the suit so as to soak up the recoil from the heavy gun.

The suit's left-hand controls operated a multiple-barrel rocket launcher system mounted on the left shoulder. This system fired both armor piercing and enhanced high-explosive warhead-guided projectiles, and featured a short-range 30 mm grenade launcher. This particular combination of firepower made the Toros the most heavily armed fighting suits in the world.

The first time the Peacekeepers' heavy infantry had encountered the Toros had been in South Africa, where the Hulks had come out second best. As a result of that experience, the Peacekeepers' powered fighting suits had recently been fitted with new 12.7 mm HV—hypervelocity—weapons and improved ceramal armor. With these upgrades, it was hoped that they would be able to hold their own when they came up against the bigger Toros.

The proof of that particular pudding, however, would truly be in the eating. There was no way to predict the outcome of combat, except after the fact. Even with the improved armor and weapons of the Hulk suits, the issue would be decided man to man and suit to suit on the battlefield today. The outcome wouldn't automatically be guaranteed to the side with the best powered fighting suits. There was a man inside each of the suits, and men won battles, not their weapons.

A THICK PALL OF SMOKE from the burning skimmers hung over the valley as the Peacekeeper Hulks moved to contact. Since they were going into action against other powered fighting-suit heavy infantry, the light infantry grunts were not accompanying them. They were being held in reserve either to reinforce the Hulks if they stepped in it again or to exploit any holes they punched in the hostile formation.

At the mouth of the valley, the first of the Toro suits appeared through the smoke and haze. They also had left their light infantry forces safely behind them. This would be fighting-suit-to-fighting-suit combat, a clash of armored Titans like a battle from ancient Greek mythology. Lightning bolts would fly from their fists, the earth would shake, and lesser men would cower with fear.

The clash began slowly as the combat giants maneuvered for the best opening positions. The Toros fought in three-suit sections where the Hulks usually fought in pairs. Even had they been equally matched, that alone would have given the advantage to the Argies. To even the odds a bit, the Hulks were double-teaming this time. It reduced their effective strength, and they were outnumbered already, but it was their best chance to overcome their better-armed adversaries.

Within seconds the firing began. Rosemont saw one of the Bravo Hulks take a long burst of Argie 20 mm fire and go down. Even with the improved armor protection, it was a repeat of the South African fiasco when the Hulks had been so badly outgunned.

The downed Hulk, however, rolled his disabled suit over into a firing position and laced the victorious Toro with a long burst of 12.7 mm HV fire. The hypervelocity rounds tore into the hostile heavy and stopped him in his tracks. One round punched completely through the fighting suit, as well as its operator, and hit the power pack. The resulting explosion spread pieces of the Toro and operator over a wide area.

The disabled Hulk was trying to drag his damaged suit to cover when another Toro blasted him to smoking wreckage. He was in turn knocked out by the Hulk's teammates as the battle dissolved into a melee.

Both sides were taking heavy casualties in the initial contact, but the most serious were in the ranks of the Bravo Company Bulls. They were the Hulk com-

pany who had come off second best in their first en-
counter with the Toros in South Africa, and the Bulls
were anxious to even the score. It looked as if they had
been a bit overanxious, though. In their haste to
avenge their earlier defeat, they charged deep into the
attacking Toro formation.

The Bulls' fighting suits had been artistically em-
blazoned with a dull brown bull's head on their front
plates. The bull's head was down as if charging an enemy, his red-rimmed nostrils flared and breathing
smoke, and the arching yellow horns were tipped with
dripping red. Their normally camouflaged individual
tactical numbers had been rendered in white on the
bull's forehead.

The bull's-head markings were great for esprit de
corps, but also made the Hulks better targets for hostile fire. Major Tom Schaffer, the Bulls' company
commander, was one of the first to fall to the Toro's
concentrated fire. Enraged at losing their popular
commander, the Bulls pressed the attack, their
12.7 mm HV machine guns and rocket launchers
blazing.

The Toro advance staggered under the determined
assault but did not break. Though the Bulls threw
themselves again and again against the TASA line,
they could not break through. This was one time that
sheer valor could not overcome numbers. Forced to
withdraw, the Bulls pulled back and settled down to
holding their ground and slugging it out at long range.

While Bravo Company was having a particularly
rough time of it, the Alpha Company Hulks weren't

doing all that much better on their side of the valley. From what Rosemont could follow on his tacscreen, both companies were trading suit for suit with the Argies. Most of the Hulks' hits, however, were only disabling while the hostiles were being killed. Normally that would be good news, but the problem with that ratio today was that, as always, the Peacekeepers were badly outnumbered. If they continued to trade one for one that way, they would run out of Hulk suits a long time before the TASA forces ran out of Toros.

Seeing his Hulks in serious trouble, the force commander flashed orders for the light infantry grunts to go in to support the Hulks. The grunts could not go head-to-head with the hostile powered suit infantry and survive. But, just the way they did when they had to face tanks, they could make their presence felt. A grunt hiding in the weeds with a Long Lash fire-and-forget antitank missile launcher in his hands was not to be taken lightly. Particularly when he was pissed off, and the Peacekeepers were pissed off.

ROSEMONT ACKNOWLEDGED the colonel's orders to commit one of his platoons to the battle in the valley. Though Sullivan's First Platoon was closer to the battle zone, he decided to send Stuart and his Second Platoon grunts in to aid the Hulks. This was the kind of David-and-Goliath operation that the would-be Southern cavalier got off on.

"Bold Cowboy, Bold Lancer," he transmitted to Stuart. "Stone Tower wants you to go down there and give the Bravo Bulls a hand. Charlie Company Grunts will be on your left, Bold Thunder will be on call for fire support, and Hook Talon's standing by for dust off. Stand by for taclink update."

"Affirm," Stuart answered. "Flash it."

"Cowboy, good copy," he said when the new troop dispositions appeared on his tacscreen.

"Good luck, Lancer out."

Jeb Stuart flicked over to his platoon secure frequency and keyed his mike implant. "Okay, people," he said. "Listen up. Stone Tower wants us join the party. The Hulks have run into a little more than they can handle, and we're going to try to cut down the odds for them. We've practiced this many times before and we can do it. Remember, the bigger they are, the harder they fall."

One of the grunts keyed his mike implant and started softly chanting, "War! War! War!"

Stuart grinned behind his helmet visor. They might be known as the Peacekeepers, but every man and woman in the United States Expeditionary Force knew what their real job was. They kept the peace by waging bloody war. The peace wasn't secure until the last hostile was facedown in the dirt with a Peacekeeper combat boot on the back of his neck.

More voices joined in the anonymous chant, "War! War! War!"

Stuart keyed his mike again. "All Cowboy elements, this is Bold Cowboy. Move out!"

With the platoon broken down into five-man hunter-killer teams, Stuart attached himself to the Cowboy Tango Alpha team. The team leader was a

veteran sergeant who went by the name "Mom," and
his grunts were all well trained in antiarmor tactics. It
would have been hard to find a better team to lead
against the Toros.

As they worked their way down to the far right flank
of the battle zone, Stuart kept a sharp eye out for any
signs of hostile fighting suits that might have broken
through the lines. If the Toros got past the Hulks and
slammed into the light infantry positions, there'd be
hell to pay.

A lone Toro, either hunting on its own or separated
from the rest of his section, appeared through the
smoke and brush heading directly toward them. Slipping into a shallow gully, Stuart's team fanned out to
face the Toro. It showed no signs of having seen them,
and Stuart wanted it to stay that way. He motioned for
the team's missile gunner to take it out.

Raising his Long Lash missile launcher to his
shoulder, the gunner locked the Toro in his sights.
When he heard the acquisition tone in his earphones,
he pulled the trigger. The Long Lash left the launcher
with a whoosh and, streaking flame from its exhaust,
headed for the Toro. Since it was a fire-and-forget
missile, the gunner immediately dropped the empty
launcher and ducked back down.

Stuart watched the missile streak for the Toro and
considered the matter concluded. Before the missile
struck, he saw a burst of flame and smoke appear low
on the Toro's chest. He swore, stunned to see the
antitank missile explode harmlessly in midair, ten
meters in front of the Toro.

The bastard had been fitted with a reactive defense system. It was common to find heavy armored vehicles fitted with these missile-defeating, controlled-explosive devices, but he had never even heard of them being used on powered fighting suits. As heavy as the Toro was, however, it could soak up the back blast almost as well as a small armored vehicle.

The back blast of the reactive defense system rocked the Toro back on his heels. When the smoke cleared, he was still on his feet and swinging his short-barreled 20 mm machine cannon around to bear on his tormentors.

"Oh, shit!"

"Cover!" Mom yelled over the comlink.

The 20 mm fire chewed into the far bank as Stuart's team dived for cover in the bottom of the gully. The Long Lash hadn't worked on this guy, but Stuart had more than one trick up his sleeve. With his battlefield sensors and laser designator taclinked to Hank Rivera's fire direction center—FDC—Stuart was able to instantly call on the weapons platoon's heavy firepower.

"Bold Thunder, Cowboy Tango Alpha," he called over his comlink. "We need a Matador ASAP."

"Thunder, affirm. Flash it, Tango Alpha."

Stuart keyed his comlink and sent the target data to the FDC.

"Thunder, good copy." the FDC answered. "One Matador on the way. Keep your heads down."

The Matador warhead for the 120 mm rocket mortar rounds was a relatively recent development specifically designed to take out fighting suits and light armored vehicles. Guided to the target by a laser designator, the round detonated two hundred meters above the target and rained a dozen armor-piercing submunitions down upon it.

The sky was shattered when the Matador arrived. The sharp crack of the primary detonation sounded loud over the roar of the battlefield. The multiple detonations of the submunitions followed immediately. One of the little bombs exploded on top of the Toro's power-pack compartment. The blast set off the power-pack, and the resulting explosion shredded the massive fighting suit.

When the last of the pieces of Toro suit and its operator stopped falling, Stuart stuck his head above the embankment and looked around. One Toro down, several more to go. He swung his arm overhead in the traditional follow me signal, and the team moved out again.

6

In the Valley—10 November

As the sun slipped behind the hill and darkness fell over the Passo Fundo Valley, the battle of the powered fighting-suit giants ground to a halt. Even though the suits could fight at night as well as they could during the day, both the Toros and the Hulks were exhausted and their ammunition was running dangerously low. Almost as if my mutual agreement, both sides started slowly withdrawing the bulk of the remaining heavies at the same time.

As the Hulks pulled back from the killing fields to resupply, repower and regroup, the grunts moved forward to hold their positions. Jeb Stuart moved his hunter-killer team up to positions along the forward edge of the battle area and dug in. He sure as hell wasn't sorry to see the fighting wind down for the day. He had lost three men in the platoon so far, and another half dozen were wounded. Fortunately only one of his wounded had been seriously hurt, but she was not expected to survive her wounds.

On the balance, with the help of the weapons platoon's Matadors, his hunter-killer teams had managed to bag three Toros. They had also disabled a fourth and had assisted the Bravo Bulls in making several more kills. As far as he was concerned, it was not what he would call a particularly good box score. Trading lives for lives on the battlefield did not appeal to him. As Mick Sullivan was found of quoting, "No one ever won a war by dying for his country. He won it by making some other poor son of a bitch die for his."

In Stuart's books that went double when it wasn't even your country you were dying for. As a Peacekeeper officer and professional soldier, Jeb Stuart always tried to keep a dispassionate mind about his work. No matter how hard he tried, he almost always failed. He simply could not be dispassionate about watching his people die in battle. Particularly a battle as senseless as this one. Fighting a war over trees didn't make much sense to him. He was fully aware that the rain forest was not the real reason for the war—human greed was. But it was easier to blame the trees than it was human nature.

Once the battlefield was secured, the combat medic teams finished recovering the casualties from both sides. Even though they had been on the battlefield from the beginning, there were still more than enough casualties to keep them busy for several hours. The first to be treated, of course, were those whose bio readouts still showed signs of life.

The graves registration teams followed behind the medics, recovering the bodies of the dead. Like the medics, they provided their services to the casualties of both sides. Once the combatants were dead, they were accorded equal treatment and equal honor. The TASA dead would be turned over to the UN team for return to their nations of origin at the first opportunity. The Peacekeeper fallen would be immediately flown back to the United States on the empty Valkyries.

IN THE HALLS of the United Nations building, the news of the battle in the Passo Fundo Valley did little to calm anyone. If anything, it only excited passions that were already at a fever pitch. Those who had backed the TASA attack were bitterly disappointed that once more it appeared that the Peacekeepers had ruled supreme over yet another battlefield. Those who had sided with Brazil against what they saw as naked TASA aggression condemned the Argentinean-led alliance in the harshest terms.

To prevent further outbreaks of physical violence between the delegates, the UN security police had stationed themselves in the chambers. The diplomats could scream at one another, but there would be no more fistfights in the building dedicated to world peace.

The fight in the United Nations was nothing, though, compared to the uproar that began when the first holos of the battle were shown on the CNN newscasts.

As always happened anytime the Peacekeepers were deployed, the CNN holovee news teams had shown up hot on their heels. From their own network-owned

UAVs and light armored skimmers, they taped the last part of the battle and its aftermath. The cameras zoomed in on the twisted wreckage of the TASA vehicles, lingering on the burned corpses of the crewmen. When they had recorded enough charred meat, they switched to taping the disabled powered fighting suits.

The wreckage of man and machine that was a fallen fighting suit was even more fascinating than mere human death. There was something about the shattered grandeur of the fallen combat giants that never failed to fascinate their audiences. If the CNN news crews knew nothing else, they knew how to satisfy their audience.

Along with the shots of the burned-out vehicles and the corpses, the CNN holovee newscasts that evening showed a thick pall of dense black smoke hanging over the valley. This aspect of the battle immediately drew harsh criticism from the Greens, who trumpeted ecological doom and gloom. They instantly appeared with extensive charts and graphs showing how much environmental damage would result from the pollution caused by the smoke. Initially they had screamed the loudest for military action to protect the rain forest, but now they demanded that the fighting be stopped instantly.

But it is always far easier to start a war than it is to end one. The Greens had gotten what they had asked for and now they were going to have to live with it. The gods of war had been awakened and they were not ready to go back to sleep just yet.

EVEN THOUGH the TASA assault had been halted for the moment, there was no indication that the Argentineans were ready to call off their invasion. In fact, the satellite Intel readouts indicated that they were rushing reinforcements into the battle zone as fast as they could under the cover of darkness.

Darkness was not an effective cover on a modern battlefield, but old habits die hard. Regardless of recon satellites, night-vision gear, sensors and the entire array of technology that had been developed to turn the night into day, wars were still fought by men. And men remembered the night as being a shield from their enemies.

The rocket artillery batteries on both sides dueled periodically throughout the night. Most of the firing was HIF, harassment and interdiction fire, designed to keep the other side from getting too comfortable. As soon as one of the batteries fired a barrage, they had to pack up and relocate quickly. Since each side was probing the sky over the battlefield with counterbattery radar, for a gun to stay put after firing was to risk having it obliterated by counterbattery fire. CB radar could pinpoint an enemy artillery gun by following the trajectory of its projectiles back to their point of origin in under a minute.

WHILE THE ARTILLERY dueled overhead, Rosemont had his recon teams out in his sector of the battlefield. Their mission was to supplement the Intel coming in from both the airborne Bats and the satellites by providing a closer look at the hostiles' dispositions.

Kat Wallenska slid through the pampas grass like a shadow under the moonless sky. Her chameleon suit had turned to shades of gray-black, she wore black combat cosmetics on her hands, and the silver skull earring had been exchanged for the matt black one she carried with her for night work. All blacked out, the Kat was in her element again.

Her path was taking her across the front line a klick forward of the known Argie positions. Strider Alpha's mission tonight was to recon the hostile positions and try to map out exactly where they were so the weapons platoon could drop a few EHE—enhanced high explosive—warhead surprises on them a little later.

So far, it had been a routine recon and it was almost finished. The TASA forces were keeping to their holes and apparently had not sent patrols forward of their edge of the battle area. That was fine with Kat, as she was not in the mood for a pissing contest tonight. She just wanted to get this shit over with and go back to grab some much-needed sack time before tomorrow's festivities commenced.

As she prepared to turn back toward the Peacekeepers' lines, a faint reading flashed across her sensor screen. She stopped and faced the Argie positions again, and there it was, a faint ripple in her magnetic anonomy detector—MAD—readout. It wasn't a hard reading, and she wasn't able to pinpoint it.

After trying but failing to bring it in clearer, she checked her tacscreen to see if anyone else was close enough to lock on to it. One of the Second Platoon's hunter-killer teams was some five hundred meters to her left flank and slightly behind her.

"Cowboy Tango Alpha," she flashed. "Strider Alpha."

"Tango Alpha," Jeb's voice came back. "'Bout time you showed up. What do you have?"

"I'm showing a faint MAD trace in Sector Three Charlie. Do you have it, too?"

"That's a negative, Strider. I'm not getting anything in Three Charlie." That was not too surprising, considering that the sensors in the recon helmets were considerably more powerful than the ones in the grunt helmets.

"Affirm, Tango Alpha. How 'bout covering us while we go take a closer look."

"That's most affirm, Strider Alpha. We've got you covered. Go get 'em."

Leaving the rest of her team in place, Kat flashed a signal for Ironstone to follow her. For night work, few were as good as the Indian, and that included Kat herself. She hardly even noticed it when he silently slid in beside her like a shadow.

It took time for the two of them to carefully work their way forward some two hundred meters. Finding a good position, they halted and looked for the intruder again. Turning her helmet audio input up all the way, she caught a faint whining noise. Turning in the direction of the noise, she carefully scanned for the distinctive sensor traces of a fighting suit, but there was nothing. Ironstone didn't have anything on his screens, either.

Concerned that her sensors were being jammed, she called Stuart again. "Cowboy, Strider Alpha. Are you sure that you aren't picking anything up?"

"That's a big negative, Strider. I have you and the Ironman on the screen, but that's all."

"Affirm, Cowboy. Keep an eye on us, will you?"

"That's most affirm."

While Kat had great trust in her sensors and detectors, there were those times when modern technology came up short and only the baseline human senses would do. She flipped her helmet visor up, baring her face to the cool night air. She knew that she was increasing her IR signature by doing that and thus presenting a better target to whoever or whatever was out there, but she had to do it. No matter what her sensors told her, there was something out there.

There it was again, a faint rustling in the tall grass twenty meters to her right front. Slipping her night-vision goggles down over her eyes, she focused on that area and saw the tips of the grass blades gently swaying. Her helmet's sensor input filters would have ignored that particular movement, attributing it to the wind, but her eyes told her differently. Something was there.

Signaling Ironstone to stay put and cover her, she crept forward on her belly. Even though she had heard a faint mechanical whine, it sure as hell wasn't a fighting suit. Even if it had been lying on its belly, she would have seen it. There was no way you could hide a fighting suit in this terrain. It could, however, be a hostile recon grunt carrying some kind of mechanical gear, or it could be some kind of sensor she was hearing.

Ten meters farther on, she dropped to the ground when something moved out from behind a thick clump of pampas grass and stopped in the open a few meters in front of her. She froze in place, not believing what she was seeing through the goggles.

The object was some kind of robotic mechanical device. The miniature body was the size of a small suitcase and it had six legs, three on each side, allowing it to walk like an insect. A low, rounded turret mounting a variety of lenses and sensor heads was fitted in the middle of the body. The entire device was only two feet tall when it crouched unmoving on its six legs.

For some reason, the small robot did not appear on either her MAD detector or her IR sensor and, as long as it did not move, her Doppler radar didn't pick it up, either. Whatever the damn thing was made of, it had little, if any, metal in it and it didn't radiate heat.

She didn't know what in the hell it was designed to do, but she knew better than to get too close to it. In fact, as far as she was concerned, she was too close to it now.

"Ironman," she whispered over her comlink. "Do you have it?"

"I don't know what it is," he said. "But I've got it in the night scope. It looks like it's some kind of mechanical cockroach."

"Load some AP rounds and keep an eye on this thing while I back out of here. I don't like the looks of that fucker."

"AP's loaded and I've got it zeroed. Get the hell outta there, Kat."

"That's most affirm, Ironman. I'm moving now."

By the time that Kat had retreated twenty meters from the cockroach, it started moving again and followed her. Lifting up each of its legs in turn, it walked like an insect as it scurried along the ground, carefully picking its way through the underbrush and shell craters.

Ironstone followed the device through his sniper scope. When it looked as if it was getting too close to Kat, he warned her before he fired. "Drop for cover!"

When the armor-piercing 8 mm round from his sniper rifle hit the cockroach, it exploded in a blinding flash. Triangular-shaped antipersonnel pellets sprayed out from it in a fifty-meter radius. Had Kat been in the way, she would have been shredded by the blast. As it was, she had been shielded by the depression in the ground she lay in.

"Kat!" Ironstone transmitted. "You okay?"

The recon sergeant pushed herself up from the ground. "Yeah, I'm fine. But we'd better check and see if there are any more of those little bastards around here."

Now that she knew what she was facing, she set her Doppler radar to pick up even the faintest movement and saw that there were several more of the robots heading toward the Peacekeepers' positions. Getting on the horn, she called the units along the front line and warned them to be alert for the robotic bombs.

Once the Peacekeepers knew what to look for and how to deal with them, the TASA mechanical cockroaches were quickly eliminated. They were not able to capture one intact, however. One of the devices was disabled by gunfire, but when it was approached by a Hulk in his fighting suit, it self-detonated.

"Nasty little bastards," the Hulk sent back as he picked triangular pellets from his armor.

7

In the Valley—11 November

As dawn broke, it was calm over the Brazilian valley. Most of the fires had died out during the night, and only a thin film of smoke stained the clear morning sky. The wreckage of battle still littered the valley floor, but it was all TASA debris. During the night, the destroyed Hulk suits had all been collected and taken to the force maintenance area on the other side of the river.

Even though most of the recovered suits were little more than shattered hulls, parts salvaged from them could help keep the others in action when they were damaged. Also, the Peacekeepers considered it to be bad form to leave the battlefield littered with their downed equipment. Blasted hostile wreckage was left where it had been destroyed as a warning to others who would not keep the peace, but no one would ever display a Peacekeeper wreck as a war trophy.

As the sun cleared the hills overlooking the valley, the Peacekeepers held to their positions. Until they could get resupplied for renewed offensive action, they would sit tight where they were and block any further

TASA advance. The next tactical move was up to the TASA forces and it wasn't long in coming.

The sun was still climbing in the midmorning sky when the roar of tank turbines sounded at the end of the valley. Most of the force's Bats were down for routine maintenance, but the standby UAV was quickly launched and sent aloft to investigate this new development. The information it flashed back confirmed that an armored battalion, some fifty main battle tanks, was moving up the valley toward them.

Though the Peacekeepers didn't have heavy armor themselves, this was still a battle they were well equipped to fight. Every grunt and Hulk spent as much time practicing to fight tanks as they did practicing infantry tactics. Also they were well equipped with tank-killing weapons. Even the fast-moving armored skimmers could be fitted with fire-and-forget antitank missiles.

Also to their advantage was the fact that the terrain did not favor a full-scale armored assault. Though the valley floor was flat and provided good mobility for tanks, it was not very wide and narrowed toward the river to the north. The farther the TASA armor battalion advanced, the less room they would have to maneuver. They would be forced to slow down, and a slow-moving tank was a dead tank.

Once again the Peacekeepers allowed the hostile armor force to come deep into the valley. But they didn't stay in their holes and wait for them. Abandoning their positions, they quickly broke up into hunter-killer teams and moved forward to their pre-prepared positions just as the tanks began firing.

Once the grunts were in position, the Peacekeeper artillery began their long-range fire. Where the artillery had been of limited use against the Toro suits the day before, they were the centerpiece of this battle. Matador projectiles, guided to their targets by the grunt's laser designators, scored hit after hit on the charging tanks with their deadly antiarmor submunitions.

The top armor on any tank is thin, and the TASA tanks were no exception. The Matador submunitions were small, but a single hit on an engine deck could disable a tank. A hit on the top of a turret could kill the tank commander and most of his turret crew.

Rosemont kept back with the company CP and watched the battle develop on his tactical monitors. Even with the hammering they were taking from the artillery, the tanks charged on through the carnage. Mick Sullivan came over the comlink with one of his quotes: "Half a league, half a league, half a league onward. All in the valley of death rode the six hundred."

Leave it to Mick to see the bravery of the doomed TASA tankers.

As the tanks pressed their attack, the skimmers swept in on both flanks and unleashed their Long Lash missiles while running at full speed. By firing from maximum range, they didn't have the accuracy that they would have had from close range, but what kills they got added to the carnage. The tanks that were not knocked out for good were most often disabled and became prime targets for the grunts and their shoulder-fired missiles.

The final stroke was when the artillery abruptly cut off and the Bubble Tops swept in at tree-top level from three different directions. The fast-flying, highly maneuverable armed scout ships swarmed over the battlefield, their chain guns spitting 20 mm depleted-uranium armor-piercing rounds and their missile pods blazing fire.

STUNNED BY THE FEROCITY of the Peacekeeper defense, the surviving TASA tanks spun around on their tracks and laid their gun barrels over their rear decks to cover their retreat. Turbines screaming at maximum power, they headed back to their own lines at full speed. Beyond a few parting shots to speed them on their way, the Peacekeepers let them go. They had left more than half of their number burning in the valley and they would not be back anytime soon.

As the TASA armor pulled back, the Peacekeepers moved back and reoccupied their former positions. The thick smoke rising from the destroyed tanks darkened the noonday sun, and the grunts ate their lunch in the shade.

NOW THAT the TASA advance had been stopped and a front line had been established, the scattered Brazilian army had been able to reconsolidate their forces. Since they were not armed well enough to go head-to-head with the TASA forces and win, the Peacekeepers assigned them auxiliary tasks away from the front lines. One of those tasks was to provide liaison officers to the Peacekeeper units.

The morning after the tank battle, a jungle-camouflaged Brazilian army skimmer skidded to a halt in front of Rosemont's Echo Company CP. The officer in the command hatch slid his goggles up over his helmet and climbed down over the front plate. Brushing the dust from his jungle camouflage uniform, he took off his AVC helmet and replaced it with a black beret cocked over his left eye.

Rosemont had been informed of his arrival and went to meet him. The Brazilian officer stiffened to a position of attention in front of the Peacekeeper and rendered a crisp salute. "Captain Alfonzo Manoel Antonio Jose de Salazar at your service, Major."

Rosemont returned his salute. "Pleased to meet you, Captain. I'm Alexander Rosemont, the Echo Company Commander. By the way, what do I call you?"

"Spike—" Salazar grinned boyishly as he extended his hand "—they called me Spike at West Point."

Rosemont grinned back as he shook hands. "Spike it is. They call me Alex around here."

Sullivan and Ashley had walked up by then, and Rosemont introduced them. "This is Captain Thomas Sullivan, my XO, and Captain Ashley Wells, my Recon platoon leader."

Salazar took Mick's hand firmly. "Pleased to meet you, Captain."

"Call me Mick."

"I'm Spike."

When he stepped up to Ashley, the Brazilian stiffened, clicked his heels and bowed at the waist. "So very pleased to meet you, Senhora Wells." His eyes flashed up to the captain's bars on her epaulets. "Senhora Capitō Wells."

When Salazar bent over her extended hand, Sullivan flashed Rosemont a here-we-go-again look. Rosemont grinned and shrugged. Ashley had this effect on every man who ever met her. If anyone in the world would know about her effect on men, he should.

"Spike," Rosemont broke in on Salazar's reverie, "if you'd like to step into my CP, I can show you my company's dispositions."

"Oh, right, the CP." Salazar tore his eyes away from Ashley and followed Rosemont into his CP bunker.

The first thing Rosemont did was to reach into the small cooler built into his field desk and come out with two unmarked cans of cold beer. He popped the top on one and asked Salazar, "Can you use a beer to settle the dust?"

"Thank you, Alex, that would be nice."

Salazar frowned when Rosemont handed him the bare metal, unmarked can with a pull top.

"It's our own special brew," Rosemont explained. "We have it made for us at Fort Benning. It's unmarked so we don't offend any locals who have religious prohibitions against alcohol."

"You won't have a problem with that in Brazil," Spike said with a conspiratorial smile as he raised the can. *"Saúde!"*

"Cheers!"

Rosemont offered Salazar a seat as he sat at his desk. "I'm glad to have you on board, we can use you."

"How can the Brazilian army be of service to you?"

"The main thing I'm going to need from your people is some local guides who are bilingual. We have a lot of linguists in the Peacekeepers who speak Spanish, but no one who speaks Portuguese. And for some reason, we didn't run any of our people through Portuguese hypno-language training when we had the chance."

Salazar smiled and shook his head good-naturedly. "We expected that. Most North Americans think that we speak Spanish. It's close, but no cigar. We can provide men who speak both English and Spanish, as well as Portuguese."

"Also, we're going to need constant data up-links from your army units in the battle zone. The way this thing is shaping up, we could get an attack from any direction and we don't want to fire on your guys by mistake."

"That will be no problem."

"Now, what can we do for you?"

"All I need is a place to set up a small comset and maybe a hammock," Salazar replied. "I don't want to get in your way."

Rosemont took his arm. "We can do a hell of a lot better than that. I'll have the comtechs plug your gear into our comnet, and you can bunk down with me in the CP tent. We don't have a mess set up, but you can eat field rations with us."

Salazar grinned. "I've eaten Readi Heats before and I survived."

"Then you know what you're in for."

LATER THAT EVENING Rosemont and his officers hosted Captain Salazar to dinner. It wasn't much of a dinner, only issue Readi Heat field rations and coffee, but the hospitality was warm and real. Since this was the first actual break they had had since the capsule drop two days before, they took advantage of it to unwind a little.

After dinner, Salazar regaled his listeners with tales of the gauchos on the pampas and wild Indian tribes in the Amazon. As he talked, Rosemont tried to figure out a way to excuse himself and Ashley gracefully so they could be alone. Beyond scattered comlink communications, he'd had no contact with her since the early-morning capsule drop.

He leaned over and whispered in her ear. "What say you and I go look at a holomap or something."

She looked at him out of the corner of her eyes, a faint smile tugging at her mouth. Reaching down with her right hand, she tapped an affirmative reply on her comlink data pad and flashed it to him. He sent back the field code response to move out.

Sullivan saw the two of them stir and knew what they were trying to do. Turning to Salazar, he asked the Brazilian a question to give them a diversion and a chance to escape.

"Jesus," Rosemont said when they had gotten out of earshot of the others. "That guy can talk more than Mick, and I didn't think that was humanly possible. I need to give my ears a rest."

"Okay, Major," Ashley said with a smile. "Just exactly what was it that you wanted to see me about?"

He smiled back. "Well, Captain, since one of the most important jobs of a field commander is to see to the welfare of the men and women under his command, I thought I'd check in and see how you're doing."

"That's the personal-interview technique mentioned in chapter six of the combat leaders guide, isn't it?"

"Let me see—" he reached for his pocket "—I think I have my copy somewhere around here."

"Can you interview me in the dark?"

"I think I can manage it using the alternate braille technique."

She dropped her night-vision goggles down over her eyes for a moment and sought out the darkest corner of the company CP area. Taking his hand, she led him into the darkness, undoing her cammo jacket as she walked.

Their lovemaking was slow and tender, but still urgent and was made only more so by the fact that they were right in the middle of the Echo Company CP area. By now everyone who wasn't blind had figured out what was going on between the two of them, but it was considered bad manners to notice it. It was also considered good manners to steer clear of lovers in the field. If nothing else, the grunts of Echo Company were polite, and they were not interrupted.

A few minutes later Rosemont's comlink beeped, demanding his attention. The message was merely a routine Intel update from Mad Mike, but it brought the two Peacekeepers back to reality. They could take a brief time out from the war, but the war wasn't going to go away and leave them alone.

"Well, coffee break's over," he sighed. "Back on our heads."

"That's right." She sat up. "Just screw and run. If I'd have known that you were going to be one of those guys, I'd have taken my business someplace where it would be more appreciated. Maybe our gallant young Captain Salazar would be a little more attentive."

Rosemont chuckled. "You'd have to get him to shut up first. I think he's too seriously in love with his own voice to pay much attention to you."

"I don't know about that," she said, smiling. She flashed him a teasing look as she closed her cammo jacket over her breasts. "I saw how he looked at me. Maybe I could change his mind and get him interested in something else."

"You do and I'll put you up on charges of misuse of government property."

She laughed. "If you're going to be that way about it, I guess I'd better get back to the platoon. I can't stand a man who doesn't have a sense of humor."

"Since I'll have Salazar bunking with me tonight, you'd better not stop by for a nightcap. He might get the wrong idea about us Peacekeepers."

She chuckled. "He already has the wrong idea about us. He thinks that we're going to wave a magic wand and save his country from the bad guys."

Rosemont instantly got serious. "It may not be that easy this time. Force is getting a lot of input about the shit storm going on in the UN. This may only be the beginning of a real war down here where everybody gets to play."

Ash shivered. She was a professional soldier, but she fought to end wars, not to start them or to make them even worse. "I sure as hell hope not."

"So do I, Ash. So do I."

8

The United Nations—13 November

Although there was a lull on the Brazilian battlefield, that did not apply to the fight raging in the halls of the United Nations. Delegates shouted charges and countercharges across the tables and made bombastic speeches. New political alliances were made and old ones broken with every impassioned speech. Armed forces were put on alert all over Central and South America. And, as always happened, the original reasons for the war were soon forgotten as old wrongs were dusted off, oiled up and made ready for new duty. Border claims, old wars, ancient disputes and outright greed all threatened to spread the TASA-Brazil War to the rest of the continent.

Even as the battle raged in the chambers of the UN, the Peacekeepers were not idle. While the grunts dug in and fortified their positions, C-36B Valkyries flew in with new supplies of armor-killing ordnance and the rest of the force's tactical aircraft. The way this situation was shaping up, they were going to need every last bit of combat power they had at their disposal. If and when the TASA army threw their full strength against the Peacekeepers, it would not be a foregone conclusion who would win.

The Peacekeepers had been faced with insurmountable odds before, but this operation had the potential of being their Waterloo. One slipup on their part or a bad roll of the dice, and the gods of war would frown on them and they would die under an armored onslaught.

While this buildup was going on, Echo Company's recon teams were far afield, trying to help even the odds against them. Their mission was to supplement the flow of battlefield Intel from the satellites and Bats with their distinctive brand of low-tech, bare-eyeball Intelligence input. The renowned Confederate General Nathan Bedford Forrest had said that he won his battles by arriving there "firstest with the mostest." The Peacekeepers, however, planned to win by knowing the most about their enemy and knowing it first.

Kat's Strider Alpha recon team had drawn a sector in the foothills far to the west of the valley, guarding the Peacekeepers' right flank. The terrain in this part of Brazil was more densely forested than the valley they had fought in before, and the trees effectively masked the ground from aerial observation. The Bat UAVs flew regular sensor runs over the area, but even they were no substitute for a well-trained set of recon team eyeballs.

FARTHER TO THE WEST of the valley, an Argentinean convoy pulled in under the canopy formed by the towering trees. Their skimmer escort quickly fanned out to form a defensive perimeter around the eight trucks as their crews dismounted. As soon as the camouflage netting and radar-masking devices had been put in place, the canvas tops of the trucks were pulled back to reveal their cargoes. Five of the trucks carried two Toro powered fighting suits in their beds, two trucks carried the ammunition and supplies for the suits, and the last truck carried their technical-support equipment.

Because of their massive size, the Toro suits had been broken down for the cross-country movement. The suits were designed to disassemble at the waist, separating the leg and lower-back sections from the arms, head and upper body. To assemble the suit, the lower section was placed in a portable assembly cradle and stood on its massive feet. The upper section was then lowered down into the cradle and locked into place. When assembled, the Toro suits were almost three meters tall.

Once the Argentinean fighting-suit techs had assembled the first suit, they quickly powered it up and ran it through the systems check. When everything was in the green, the tech team leader called out to the Toro operators, who were helping the technicians assemble the other suits, and one young Argentinean powered-suit infantryman came to claim his Toro.

He quickly settled himself into the harness and secured the muscle sensors in place on his arms, legs, feet and hands. Snapping the armored shell closed around himself, he lowered the helmet faceplate, hit the master switch and watched as the digital readings flashed past on his faceplate screen. Satisfied that the suit was functioning properly, he took his first step.

Sensing the movement of his leg muscles through piezoelectric circuits, the suit multiplied that movement through servos and the leg took a step. To the operator, it felt as if he had taken a normal step. He had exerted no more effort to move the five-hundred-kilo fighting suit than he would have used to move his eighty-kilo naked body. With a faint whine from the servo units, the Toro suit lumbered over to the ammunition carrier trucks.

There the ammo humpers quickly filled the magazine for the 20 mm machine cannon attached to the right side of the suit and loaded rockets and grenades into launchers mounted on the left side and shoulder of the Toro.

The ammunition added another two hundred kilos to the weight of the suit, but the operator barely noticed it. The suit automatically compensated for the changes in balance and the extra weight. When he was fully loaded, he walked over to the side and, parking his suit, he dismounted to help the others assemble the rest of the Toros.

It took almost two hours for the ten fighting suits to be made fully operational. But when they were, the operators mounted their Toros and, taking up a diamond formation, the heavy infantry platoon moved off toward the east and the left flank of the Peacekeepers' positions. As part of a coordinated night attack, this one platoon would be enough to punch through the Peacekeepers' defenses and open them up to the TASA armor attacking up through the valley.

KAT WALLENSKA CROUCHED in the brush along the ridge line overlooking the valley. At her side Ironstone scanned the trees below with his helmet sensors as he ate a Readi Heat ration. The rest of the team was strung out to her left along the ridge taking a lunch break.

They had been working the hills and valleys steadily since dawn and, so far, they had found nothing of interest. That was good, but it also carried a danger. Like all professional soldiers, the recon grunts were at their best when they were in danger. In the absence of indications of hostile activity, a recon mission could all too easily become a mere walk in the park, particularly if the grunts were tired.

It was the middle of the day, and she was giving her team a needed rest so they would be sharp when they moved out again. While they were resting, she and Ironstone were keeping watch on the jungle below with both their eyes and sensors as they ate their lunch.

"You hear that?" she asked him.

Ironstone frowned and stopped chewing. "Hear what?"

She tapped the audio pickup on the side of her helmet. "I'm picking up what sounds like servo whine."

Ironstone flicked on his earphone amplifier and turned his head in the direction she was facing. He didn't hear a thing, but that was not unusual. Wallenska had the ears of a cat along with the name. If she heard something, you could bet your ass something was down there. He wadded up the empty ration pack and stuffed it back into his assault pack.

Switching on his full array of helmet sensors, he also picked up his M-41 SASR sniper rifle and turned on its variable-power, self-ranging optical scope. Sometimes nothing worked as well as amplified optics for spotting movement. Starting five hundred meters in front of the ridge, he slowly swept the scope through his full arc of vision.

A little over a thousand meters to his left, he caught a glimpse of movement through the trees on the valley floor below. A second later a jungle-camouflage-painted Toro suit broke out into the open for a moment.

"I got 'em," he said, keeping the scope on the area. "Toros. Azimuth two-ninety-three, eleven hundred meters."

As he watched, several more passed the break in the tree cover. "What in the fuck are Toros doing all the way over here?"

"They're trying to get into position so they can come in on our flank," she accurately assessed the situation. "If they do that in conjunction with a frontal attack, they'll have a good chance of breaking us up."

"It's a good move," Ironstone said admiringly. As a professional solder, he could admire a good plan even when it was the hostiles who had thought of it.

"You're damn right it is," she said. "And I'd better get some help in here to deal with those guys ASAP."

She tongued her mike implant and spoke. "Bold Strider, Bold Strider. This is Strider Alpha, over."

Instead of hearing Ashley's cool voice answering her call, all Kat heard was a hissing crackle in her earphones. Frowning, she tried again.

"Any Bold Lancer station, this is Strider Alpha, Blue Star, Blue Star, over."

When the static sounded in her ears again, she tongued her mike implant over to the force headquarters frequency. "Stone Tower Control, Stone Tower Control, this is Bold Strider. Blue Star. I say again, Blue Star, over."

Again only static sounded in her earphones. Something or someone was blocking the comlink signal, and she didn't think it was accidental. "My comlink's fucked," she said. "You try it."

"No good," he said after a moment. "Mine's dead too."

"Shit!"

After alerting the rest of the team, Kat and Ironstone continued to watch as the Toros broke out of the trees and crossed a small clearing. They counted ten of the fighting suits, a full platoon of heavy infantry, more than enough to cause someone heartache if they didn't know they were coming.

The first suit following behind the pointman was decorated with three gold ten-pointed stars painted on the left breast. Since three gold stars was the rank insignia of a captain in the Argentinean army, that particular Toro had to be the platoon leader. The next suit in line behind him had three chevrons and a star painted on his left breast, marking him as the platoon sergeant.

It was nice of the Argies to have clustered their command people that way. Now all she had to do was to figure out a way to kill two Toro suits with one grunt recon team and she would be able to render the flank attack leaderless. Nothing to it if she had been a holovee Peacekeeper heroine. On the holovee sagas, a Peacekeeper could whip an army armed with only a Readi Heat field-ration plastic spoon.

As it was, she was a recon sergeant with a four-man team and only one heavy weapon, Ironstone's 8 mm sniper rifle. Taking out even one of the Toros by themselves, much less two of them, was going to be a chore. And that would be possible only if they could separate one from the rest of the platoon. Taking on the entire platoon was out of the question—there were easier ways to commit suicide.

But one way or the other, something had to be done. She couldn't let the Toros simply walk past them and hit the Peacekeepers' unprotected flank. That's why she had been sent out in the first place, to protect the flank.

"Ironman," she said. "you ready to go to work?"

"Sure," he replied. "You want me to go down there and head those guys off, right?"

"Not quite. I was thinking of something a little more like trying to poke some holes in their lexan faceplates."

Ironstone raised one eyebrow. "That's only going to piss them off. You trying to get me killed, woman?"

"Since I can't get in contact with anyone to give us a hand, we've got to do something. We can't just sit on our asses up here and blow kisses as they walk past us."

The Indian sniper looked up into the clear sky. His Comanche warrior instincts surfaced and told him that every warrior reached this moment at one time or other and he would face it the same way his ancestors had.

"Well," he said, "the sun's shining, so it's a good day to die."

Kat laughed. "Every day in the force is a good day to die, Ironman, didn't you know that?"

"That's most affirm, Kat Woman," he said, smiling. "Let's go do it."

"Don't you want to hear what I have in mind first?"

He shook his head, the smile on his face stretching the war stripes on his cheeks. "Nope, it doesn't matter. I'm just going to go down there and get myself killed."

"You get yourself killed, asshole, and I swear to God I'll bring you up on charges."

Ironstone shook his head slowly. "Sorry, Kat, that won't work this time. I'm going to get myself killed heroically today and you can't court-martial a hero. It's simply not done, you know."

Kat found herself grinning in return. When Ironstone started playing the heroic Indian warrior, the best thing to do was to go along with him. It was his way of dealing with a bad situation and, since it seemed to work for him, it was good enough for her.

"Whatever you say, Ironman, but I won't put you in for a medal if you get killed. No fucking way."

"BOLD LANCER," Ashley's voice came in over Rosemont's headphones. "Bold Strider."

"Lancer, go."

"Strider, I've lost contact with Strider Alpha. She's missed two routine comchecks, and I can't raise her or anyone else on the team."

Rosemont called up his tacscreen and punched in Kat's last reported position. Her team had been at the far western end of her sector the last time she had checked in. But that had been over an hour ago, and she could be almost anywhere in her sector by now.

"Do you have contact with Strider Bravo and Charlie?"

"That's affirm, Lancer, and they can't get through to her, either."

"Do you have air assets with you at this time?" he asked.

"Affirm, I'm launching a Bubble Top now."

"Lancer affirm, keep me posted."

There were dozens of reasons for Kat to be out of communication, but he had a bad feeling about this one. The Argies had been much too quiet lately and they could be trying to pull some kind of flank attack. Following his hunch, he flashed a tac update reporting Strider Alpha's silence to the force ops center. Mad Mike was also concerned and requested that he be kept informed.

KAT DIDN'T HAVE anything fancy in mind this afternoon. She didn't have enough people or firepower on hand for fancy. She did think, however, that she and Ironstone had a fair chance of taking out the two Toro command suits from ambush. With them out of action, it might make it difficult for the others to carry out their mission. The TASA military system did not encourage thinking on the part of its rank-and-file troops. Their troops had guts, but without their officer and NCO to give them orders, they could probably falter at a critical moment.

Also if the Toro command suits were responsible for whatever was jamming their comlinks, zeroing them would allow Kat to call back to get some help dealing with the rest of them.

It sounded good in theory, but they still had to take out two five-hundred-kilo fighting machines with a bad attitude, and they had little more than their rifles to do it with. But as Ironstone had proven in South Africa, the Toros were vulnerable if you knew how to take them down.

Quickly briefing the rest of the team on what they planned to do, Kat and Ironstone dropped their combat packs and double-checked their weapons and ammo loads. Where they were going, the packs would only get in the way. If they pulled this off, they could come back for the packs. If they didn't, they wouldn't need them where they would be going next.

9

In the Jungle—13 November

Kat and Ironstone managed to work their way down the side of the ridge without being seen by the Toros. They had angled off far to the right so they were well out in front of the advancing machines when they reached the valley floor. The vegetation there was thick enough to hide them until they wanted to be seen.

The rest of the Strider Alpha team had been left up on the ridge line to provide fire support for their two-grunt hunter-killer operation. But if this didn't work out, they had orders to get the hell out immediately and save themselves. There was no reason for all of them to commit suicide today.

"How do you want to do this?" Kat asked. Now that they were down here, she was beginning to have second thoughts about their chances of pulling this off. The Ironman was the only grunt she knew who had ever taken out a Toro suit with a rifle, so she would be glad to defer to his judgment on this particular matter.

"Let me find a place with a good field of fire, and then you go off to my side for an L-shaped ambush," he said. "Then if the guys on the ridge can get them to turn around, I should be able to find a couple of vulnerable points to try to put the AP rounds in."

"Just like you did in South Africa, right?"

"Something like that."

The last time he had done it, however, he had spent a long time in the hospital recovering from the damage the Toro had done to him in return. Also he had only been up against one Toro suit then. Going up against ten of them would get him a long look at the inside of a body bag. But as Kat had said, every day in the force was a good day to die. He was wearing fresh war paint today and, since he had been ready to die since the day he had joined the force, he had better get about doing it.

A quick recon of the valley floor revealed a partial clearing along the route the Toros were taking. The undergrowth in the area was fairly thick, but it only rose to about a meter in most places. Since the Toro suits were almost three meters tall, when they entered the clearing he should have no trouble getting a clear shot at their upper torsos.

Dropping Kat off at a point on the ridge-line side of the clearing, the sniper took a position fifty meters away at the far side of the clearing. Settling in behind a huge fallen log, he loaded the AP magazine into his rifle. After chambering the first round, he changed the setting on his scope to match the ammunition he was firing.

The 8 mm armor-piercing round had a 5 mm core of tungsten carbide inside its copper ballistic jacket. Since the bullet was lighter than the standard ball round and had a higher powder load, it had a higher muzzle velocity and a flatter trajectory. Because of this, Ironstone had to switch his scope over to the AP mode to match the round's ballistics. He had only the one magazine of the 8 mm armor-piercing ammunition in his pouches, twenty-five rounds, and almost every shot would have to find a vulnerable point in the fighting suits if the plan was going to work.

Though the comlink frequencies were being blocked, the grunts' tacscreens still worked. Linking with the grunts on the ridge, Ironstone was able to see the Toros as they moved into the clearing. As he had hoped, the two command suits were still leading the formation. As with the rest of their forces, the TASA heavy infantry was heavy on equipment but short on combat experience. To better control their troops, the officers and NCOs had to personally lead them everywhere they went. That was fine with Ironstone because he only wanted the two leaders anyway. They were the ones who would have the jamming devices, and with them gone, they should be able to use their comlinks to call for help.

At his signal, the grunts on the ridge-line opened up on the rear of the Toro formation with everything they had. Two of them had 30 mm grenade launchers mounted on their LARs and added the punch of the small EHE grenades to the fury of fully automatic 5 mm fire. Even so, their fire was not heavy enough to damage the TASA fighting suits.

It did manage to get their attention, and—as Ironstone had anticipated—the Toros responded violently to the ambush. Their diamond formation broke up as they faced about and lumbered for cover at the edge of the clearing. A storm of 20 mm fire blasted the ridge line as a pair of Toros unleashed their machine cannons on the recon team. A sharp cry of pain over Kat's earphones told her that one of her grunts had taken a hit.

One man had been hit, but the tactic had worked. The Toros had turned around to face the grunts to their rear, and the back of the platoon leader's suit helmet filled Ironstone's scope. Since a fighting suit's rear armor was usually thicker than the frontal armor, he decided to try a square-on head shot and see if he could pierce the back of the Toro's helmet.

Holding his sight picture, he squeezed off his first shot. To his dismay, the AP round bounced off the ceramal armor and whined away into the jungle. The Toro started turning in his direction, and he fired again only to have this round ricochet away, as well.

The Toro was almost facing him and was bringing his 20 mm machine cannon to bear when he fired a third round. This time the 8 mm armor-piercing bullet hit exactly at the juncture of the Toro's bulletproof lexan faceplate and the ceramal armor of the helmet. The round's copper ballistic jacket spalled off between the lexan and ceramal, leaving the chisel-pointed 5 mm tungsten carbide core free to penetrate deeper.

The AP core punched through the weak point and tore a bloody furrow midway across the operator's face. It hit directly under his right cheekbone, cut across his upper lip and nicked the bottom of his nose before lodging itself in the padding on the inside of the other side of the helmet. The wound wasn't fatal, but being a face wound, it was painful and very bloody.

Fighting to breathe through the blood, the Toro officer panicked and opened his faceplate. With the lexan faceplate out of the line of fire, Ironstone's next shot took him in the bridge of the nose.

The Argentinean's skull wasn't hard enough to cause the ballistic jacket to separate from the AP core, but it didn't matter. The bullet drilled through his brain before blowing out the back of his head, piercing the helmet liner and stopping against the armor at the back of the helmet.

The Argentinean captain was dead before his Toro suit hit the ground.

The Toro platoon sergeant was a veteran and didn't panic when he saw his officer go down. Turning toward Ironstone's position to present his thick frontal armor to the sniper's fire, he brought his 20 mm cannon to bear and triggered off a long burst. The machine cannon was feeding a deadly mix of EHE and AP ammunition that tore into the log the sniper was hiding behind.

Wood splinters and explosive shell fragments tore into the lexan armor inserts of his chameleon suit, but didn't penetrate. If one of those rounds found him, however, he'd be dog meat.

Kat saw the Toro blasting Ironstone's position and sprang into action. Her LAR leveled, she jumped out from her hiding place and unleashed a stream of 5 mm fire. The light-caliber rounds ricocheted off the suit's armor like BBs, but she kept firing, hoping to draw attention away from Ironstone and give him a chance to escape.

The Toro did spin around to take care of Kat, but Ironstone didn't run for cover when he had the chance. Instead, he zeroed in on the rear of the Toro's right knee joint and fired. When the first round seemed to have no effect, he fired again and again. One of the rounds penetrated and cut through the hydraulic lines controlling the suit's right leg.

With the sudden loss of hydraulic pressure, the leg locked in the extended, default position, but the Toro stayed on his feet. The sight of the towering, massive powered fighting suit hopping around stiff legged would have been comical were it not for its 20 mm machine cannon blazing fire at Kat.

She was running flat out, dodging behind every tree she passed. So far, she was moving faster than the crippled Toro could bring his cannon to bear, but if she faltered, she'd be zeroed.

Quickly zooming his scope in on the Toro's other leg, Ironstone tried to duplicate his earlier lucky shot. When he couldn't repeat that shot, he switched his aim to the Toro's left shoulder-mounted rocket launcher.

After feeling three of Ironstone's shots bounce off the armored shielding of his launcher, the Toro decided to go back and finish him off. When he tried to turn again, however, the suit's stiffened leg got hung up in the brush. In trying to jerk it free, he used too much force, and when the legs disentangled, he toppled over onto the ground.

Standing up for a better shot, Ironstone saw that the Toro's left armpit joint was exposed. He fired, and the 8 mm AP round tore through the unprotected joint and drilled into the TASA sergeant's shoulder, continuing on to sever the jugular vein as it angled down into his chest.

The Argentinean vainly tried to raise his 20 mm, but the sudden loss of blood defeated him. The cannon fell back to the ground as he died.

Ironstone dashed out in the direction he had last seen his partner running. "Kat! Kat," he shouted.

"Over here, Ironman," he heard over his comlink.

"Where are you?"

A slightly battered Kat walked out of the brush, still breathing heavily from her close call.

"You hit?"

"I'm okay," she growled. "Let me see if we can get some help with the rest of these bastards."

"That's fine with me," Ironstone replied. "I've enjoyed about all of this shit I can stand for one day."

"Bold Lancer, Bold Lancer," Kat called. "This is Strider Alpha. Blue Star. I say again, Blue Star. Over."

"Strider Alpha, this is Lancer, go." Rosemont's welcome voice sounded in her earphones.

"This is Strider Alpha. I have a platoon of Toros heading your way at Hotel sector three-six-two and I need gunship support ASAP. Also, we've taken casualties and I need a priority Dustoff at this location."

"Lancer, copy Toros at Hotel Three Six Two and you need a Dustoff ASAP."

"Strider affirm."

"Keep your head down, Kat, the gunships and Dustoff are on the way."

"That's most affirm, Lancer. Strider out."

"Okay," she told Ironstone. "The gunship's on the way, so let's get the hell outta here before the rest of those bastards come after us."

ASHLEY WELLS was in an armed Bubble Top flying a search pattern over the southern part of Strider Alpha's recon sector when she intercepted Kat's call to Rosemont. Punching in the coordinates Kat had given, she flashed the position up on the nav screen and saw that she could get there several minutes before the other gunships. In such a situation, a few minutes could be an eternity.

"Strider Alpha, this is Bold Strider," she called to her recon team leader.

"Alpha go."

"Strider, I'm airborne with ordnance, flash me a target up-link."

"Alpha, affirm. Stand by for up-link."

"Strider, good copy," Ashley said when the ten red diamond pips of hostile targets appeared in her tacscreen. "Keep your heads down, we're coming in. ETA zero-five."

"Alpha affirm," Kat sent back. "Be advised that it looks like they're packing some kind of triple-A missile in their launchers."

"Strider, affirm. We'll keep an eye out."

The Bubble Top's skids kissed the tops of the trees on the way in to Kat's location. In the left-hand seat, Ashley slaved the weapons computer to her helmet and saw the sight pips and status data flash up on her tac-screen.

"What are you doing?" the pilot asked when she swung the weapons controls over to her side of the cockpit.

"You just fly this fucker and I'll shoot for you," Ash snapped.

"Whatever you say, Captain." The pilot knew better than to argue with Ash-and-Trash Wells. Not only would she kick his ass if he did, but she was also the second-best air-to-ground gunner in the force. Only Gunner Thompson had better scores, and the competition between the two was fierce.

Ash dialed in the 20 mm depleted-uranium AP ammo feed for the chain gun and preselected the Long Lash missiles on the pylons to recognize Toro powered fighting suits as their primary targets. Flexing her fingers, she wrapped her hands around the twin grips of the Bubble Top's weapons controls. Her thumbs rested on the missile pylon buttons, her right trigger finger controlled the chain gun, and her left, the grenade launcher. She was ready to go to work.

As KAT HAD SUSPECTED, the death of the two Toro commanders had left the other eight suits leaderless. Nevertheless, they hadn't been rendered any less dangerous. Forming up into their usual three-man combat teams, they fanned out in the brush to track down their tormentors.

Cut off from the ridge line and the other grunts, Kat and Ironstone fled deeper into the trees. Twenty mm cannon fire shredded the trees around them as they ran, but they didn't even try to stop and fight. Ironstone had been lucky twice, but the third time might not be a charm.

WHEN THE SPEEDING Bubble Top approached the ridge line, the pilot dropped down as low to the ground as he could and extended his MAADS, the rotor mast acquisition and detection system. Extending a meter above the rotor disk when it was fully deployed, this sensor system allowed him to look over the top of the ridge without exposing the scout ship to the Toro's observation and fire.

"Strider Alpha, Ash. I'm zero-two out and ready to go to work. Give me a taclink update."

"Kat, affirm. Up-linking now."

"Good copy, I've got the targets. Keep your heads down, we're coming in."

With her tacscreen linked with Kat's helmet, as well as the MAAD sensors, Ashley had two sets of targets to work on. Seeing the grunts on the unprotected ridge line under fire from a pair of Toros, she decided to take them out first.

Heeding Kat's warning about the Toros being armed with antiaircraft missiles, she set up the attack while the Bubble Top was hiding behind the ridge line. Using the mast-mounted targeting system, she quickly programmed the missiles to find their two targets.

Popping up only far enough to clear the pyloned missile pods, Ashley fired and dropped back down behind the ridge in well under thirty seconds. The two antitank missiles streaked for their targets and connected a split second later. Twin explosions rocked the valley as their shaped-charge EHE warheads blasted the Toros to oblivion.

For her next targets, she chose the two Toros who were chasing Kat and Ironstone. Flying over the valley was risky because there was no place to maneuver if they fired the antiaircraft missiles Kat had reported. But it was Kat and Ironstone down there, and she owed them more than a few.

When she flashed the targets up on the pilot's screen, he looked at her as if she was deranged. Since he feared her more than the missiles, he popped up over the ridge anyway and dived down after them. The first Toro was easy; he didn't even try to defend himself as he went down under a burst of 20 mm chain gun fire. The depleted-uranium AP rounds punched through his ceramal armor as if it were soft cheese.

The second Toro tried to duke it out with his own 20 mm cannon, and Ash's pilot had to do a couple of quick doopsy-doos to keep out of his line of fire. In the end, however, Ash got him with another Long Lash missile.

By the time Ash had gotten the Toros off Kat and Ironstone, the Dustoff and the Hook Talon gunships Rosemont had dispatched arrived. While the Medevac chopper took on the wounded grunt on the ridge line, the gunships ran down and eliminated the last of the Toros. It was all over in five minutes.

10

In the Valley—14 November

With the detection and destruction of the Toro platoon attempting the flank attack, the situation in the Passo Fundo Valley settled down to a stalemate. The dueling artillery batteries sent the occasional round back and forth, and recon patrols traded small-arms fire, but there were no more major TASA attacks.

The ongoing battle in the chambers of the UN had also stabilized somewhat, but that was not necessarily good news. The delegates stopped their bickering only long enough to issue an injunction prohibiting the Peacekeepers from launching a counterattack to drive the TASA forces back behind the Argentinean borders and destroy them. For the moment all they were authorized to do was sit where they were and block any further advances into Brazilian territory.

Protests by both the Brazilian government and the United States to at least restore the original national boundaries did no good. Argentina had powerful friends in the UN.

In spite of the United Nations' clampdown on the Peacekeepers, the Argentineans continued to mass their forces in the sector of southern Brazil they had occupied. Force Intel kept a close watch on the buildup. From all indications, it was felt that sooner or later they would unleash another lightning attack and try to punch through the Peacekeepers' lines to continue their drive deeper into the heart of Brazil. Normally, under these tactical circumstances, the Peacekeepers would strike first to keep that from happening, but with the UN injunction in force, their hands were tied.

Needless to say, this situation did not sit very well with the men and women of the USEF. They were the Peacekeepers, the most ass-kickingest military force that had ever worn combat boots. Sitting on their butts in static defensive positions while politicians jacked their jaws was not their style of doing business. As far as they were concerned, the only thing worse than fighting a war was not fighting it. They wanted to get in there, get their buckles in the dirt, kick some TASA ass, get the situation under control and go home to Fort Benning.

Now that a hold had been placed on the war, the only action anywhere in the theater was in the far western sector of Brazil, where the Peruvian TASA forces had started probing the border with small units. To prevent the TASA from gaining another foothold in the beleaguered nation, Delta Company had been sent to stabilize the situation. Currently they were fighting small units at scattered points along the border in the high Andes.

The other grunt company commanders envied the Delta Devils and wanted to get in on the action, but Rosemont was content to let them fight in the mountains. It was cold up there, and he hated fighting in the cold. So, beyond sending his grunts out to aggressively patrol along the forward-edge trace and running recon missions, the Echo Company grunts had little to do.

This forced inactivity, however, was not welcomed. Since they couldn't fight, they did what they could to amuse themselves. The portable field-shower unit became quite popular, as did the chow line at the mess tent that had been set up. Readi Heats weren't that bad, but fresh-cooked food was more than welcome.

As always, Mick Sullivan had brought his portable holodisk player and his sizable supply of laser disks and he set it up to help pass the time for the off-duty troops. The grunts had long since learned that he only brought movies made before the turn of the century and they had also learned to bring a few of their own favorites to provide a little variety.

For Ashley and Rosemont, the respite in the battle gave them an opportunity to spend more time together. Since Ash was sending only two recon teams out at any given time, she stayed back and oversaw their operations from the company CP. That also meant that she was sleeping at the CP every night. And, although she kept her own bedroll, that didn't mean that she couldn't stop off and say good-night to Rosemont before she went to sleep.

There were no hard-and-fast rules about sex in the Peacekeepers; the force command knew human nature better than that. Rather than foolishly prohibiting something that was going to occur anyway, they expected the men and women to act as the professional soldiers they were. When sexual problems did arise, they were handled as breaches of discipline or as a dereliction of duty. Even so, both Ashley and Rosemont knew that spending the night together would be stretching the nonexistent rules.

Ash and Rosemont were both well aware that this lull in the war would not, and could not, last forever. Already it had lasted longer than either one of them had even hoped that it would. The war would start again soon enough. But until it did, they would enjoy it.

IT WAS A LITTLE PAST TWO in the morning. Ashley had left around midnight, and Rosemont was in a deep sleep when he was wakened by one of the CP comtechs. "What is it?" he asked groggily.

"A Blue Star flash from the force commander, Major," the man said, his voice excited.

That brought Rosemont wide-awake instantly. Blue Star was the highest-priority message in the Peacekeeper comcode system. Something big was finally going down. "What does he want?"

"He wants you at a briefing at the force CP. A Bubble Top's en route to pick you up."

"What's its ETA?"

"Zero-two, sir."

Rosemont jammed his feet into his boots and reached for his helmet. "I'm on the way."

He had no sooner reached the chopper pad outside the CP perimeter than the blacked-out Bubble Top flared out for a landing. Rosemont scrambled into the right side of the small chopper, and the pilot lifted off even before he had finished buckling himself in.

"What's the flap?" he asked as soon as he plugged into the chopper's comlink.

"Damned if I know," the pilot answered. "All I know is that Mad Mike told me to get your ass back there as fast as I could turn the rotors."

All the way back, the Bubble Top flew just a few meters above the treetops. Even though he was well out of range of the TASA missiles, it never hurt for a scout-ship pilot to be cautious. A few minutes later the small chopper flared out at the blacked-out force CP landing pad.

Rosemont was unbuckled and rushing out of the door as soon as the Bubble Top's skids kissed the landing pad. Ducking to clear the chopper's still-spinning rotor blades, he ran for the ops center complex. When he walked into the CP, Rosemont realized that whatever was going on, it had to be big time. The ops center normally ran twenty-four hours a day, but it usually wasn't this crowded at this time of night. It looked as if everyone from the mess officer to the maintenance chief was there.

He elbowed his way through the crowd and spotted the operations officer at the other end of the room. LTC Taylor Michaels was chomping furiously on the dead cigar butt clamped between his teeth. His dark eyes flashed as he huddled with the force medical officer.

Colonel Jacobson looked up from his holotank when he saw Rosemont approaching and waved him over. "Rosemont," he called out. "Glad you're here. I'm pulling your people out of the line immediately."

Rosemont frowned. "What's up, sir?"

"I've got a priority mission for you," he said, his voice low. "You know that Delta Company was pulled out and sent to the Andes to cover western Brazil?"

"Yes, sir."

"Well, they've run into a real problem up there. Ninety-five percent of them are down with a genetically engineered virus, and over a dozen have already died."

Rosemont was stunned. Biological weapons were even more universally prohibited than nuclear weapons. "An engineered virus, sir?"

Jacobson nodded. "Yes, a specifically tailored biological-warfare agent that evidently is only effective at high altitudes. Apparently it was developed from a strain of flu that originated in the Himalayas in China, and we think the Han are involved."

"How the hell did it get over here, sir?"

"That's exactly what I'm sending you up there to find out." The colonel's voice was grim and determined, but when he caught the look on Rosemont's face, he quickly added, "We've got a vaccine for it, though. And you'll all get inoculated before you move out."

Rosemont looked relieved.

"And," Jacobson continued, "along with trying to track down a case of the flu with a bad attitude, you'll have another little problem to contend with."

"What's that, sir?"

"For the last two days Delta Company has been reporting that they were encountering Han mountain troops in platoon-sized units."

Rosemont whistled softly. "How the hell did Han Chinese troops get over here, sir?"

"Someone dropped the ball on this one and they slipped past us." The colonel did not sound pleased to have to admit this Intelligence failure. "Apparently the troops came in with the mining and resource teams that arrived last year, and they shipped their weapons and equipment in with the mining machinery."

Bolivia and Peru, the junior partners in TASA, shared Argentina's dreams of dominating South America. But unlike their senior partner, they were not as well off and had little to contribute to the alliance except manpower and raw materials.

When the last coca tree had been eradicated in 2018, Bolivia's and Peru's economies had completely collapsed. The little that was left after the coca was gone was completely agriculturally based. In an attempt to revive their nation's economies, the rulers of the two small nations had joined in a plan to exploit the great untapped resources of the Andes Mountains. With no capital to finance the venture, however, they had invited the Han Chinese to assist them in developing new resource-based industries.

The Han were more than willing to gain a foothold in Andean South America, as they desperately needed the raw materials it would provide. Not only were China's resources quickly becoming exhausted, but she also needed a place for her excess population and the sparsely populated Andes would do nicely.

It was well-known that the Han had been building mining facilities, smelters and metal-fabrication factories in the Andes. It was also known that they had brought large numbers of their nationals in to run these facilities. What had not been known was that the Chinese had been covertly infiltrating troops and weaponry into the region for the past year and a half. For some unknown reason, this military buildup had gone completely unnoticed. In a world where the movement of military forces was almost always a precursor to war, the oversight was criminal.

"You think the Han are responsible for the virus, sir?" Rosemont asked.

"That's the assumption," Jacobson answered. "I want you to get up there, find those bastards and put an end to this before it gets completely out of control. We have to keep an eye on the Argies here, so I can't send another company with you, but you'll have all the assets you'll need once you find the Han."

The colonel looked up and saw that the ops officer was not waiting too patiently. "Mad Mike has all the details for you and he wants you on your way ASAP, so you'd better get over there and talk to him. Good luck, Rosemont."

"Thank you, sir."

The ops officer got straight to the point when he briefed Rosemont on his mission. After going over the air assets, the on-call fire support, resupply and the dozen other operational details, he handed the company commander a thick packet of hard copies.

"Here's your mission pack," he said. "The Tilt Wings will be at your CP in less than an hour, and I need your people in the air as soon as they arrive. With or without the virus, if the Han get loose in that area, we'll never get them gathered up."

"That's most affirm, sir. We're on the way."

"Get there quickly, Rosemont," Mad Mike growled around the dead cigar butt in his mouth. "Those bastards have had twelve hours to steal a march on us."

"You got it, sir."

WHEN ROSEMONT GOT BACK to his company CP, he found it a beehive of activity. The low-light illumination system had been activated so the grunts could go about their tasks without having to wear their night-vision goggles. The supply personnel were stacking ammunition crates and ration boxes next to the landing pad for the Tilt Wing loads. The men and women were hurrying about their assignments as if it were four o'clock in the afternoon, not four in the morning.

At the aid station, he found the force medics already administering the flu antibodies to the sleepy grunts. He cut in at the head of the immunization line and took his place in front of the medic with the inoculation gun.

"Fill 'er up, regular," he quipped as he rolled up his cammo sleeve.

Even though he had heard that ancient joke several times already, the medic grinned as he pulled the trigger. Since Major Rosemont was a good guy, he didn't give the gun that slight little twist that would cause the pressurized vaccine to tear into his muscles and give him a sore arm for a week. He reserved that special technique for officers who unwisely gave him a hard time.

"What's our status, Top?" Rosemont asked First Sergeant Ravenstein as he rolled his sleeve down.

The Hawk consulted his data pad. "We'll be ready to move out in a little less than half an hour, Major. Right now we're waiting for Charlie Company to move up and take over our positions."

"Flash 'em and tell 'em to get a move on it ASAP, Top. The Old Man wants us up in those mountains yesterday."

"That's affirm, sir."

While Top Ravenstein departed to speed up the process, Rosemont went to gather his own gear together. As he had expected, the CP tent had already been pulled down, but his equipment had been laid aside for him. As he prepared for combat, he looked around for Ashley, but couldn't find her. But it was just as well. Their time off was over, and they both had their jobs to do now.

THE FIRST of the AV-18 Tilt Wing assault transports arriving to lift Echo Company to their new AO came in low and fast over the treetops. Even though he was well back from the TASA front lines, the pilot was taking no chances on getting a missile stuffed up his tail pipe. Two OH-39 Bubble Top armed scout ships accompanying the assault transport orbited above the PZ as the Tilt Wing touched down.

The grunts were standing by and quickly loaded the first ship. As soon as it lifted off, its wings repositioning to level flight, another one settled down in its place. Within minutes the entire company had been loaded up and was in the air for the four-hour flight to their new AO high in the Andes Mountains.

11

In the Air—15 November

Even with the assault transport's heaters going full blast, it was cold inside the Tilt Wing as the aircraft gained altitude as it headed up into the Andes Mountains. Rosemont shivered and sincerely wished he was back in the muggy Brazilian jungles with the rest of the force. Possibly he would be sitting on his dead ass back there, but at least he'd be warm and he hated to be cold.

Also, if he was honest with himself, he knew that he would miss the extra warmth that Ashley had brought him the past few nights. He had enjoyed that all-too-brief interlude more than he had words to describe. Now that they were operational again, it would be a long time before he felt her beside him again. Then he pushed those thoughts from his mind and got back to the matter at hand.

For this operation, Rosemont rode the last Tilt Wing in the formation rather than flying in the lead aircraft. This way, he could act as the C-and-C ship, command and control, and direct the aerial insertions of the grunt platoons into their landing zones before he went on to where he would establish his new CP base camp.

The tactical monitor in front of him displayed the positions of the other Tilt Wing assault transports in the flight carrying the grunt platoons. It also showed the positions of the Tac Air gunships and Bubble Tops keeping formation with them. A second wave of assault transports was following half an hour behind them, carrying Hank Rivera's weapons platoon and a battery of Thunderbolt antiaircraft missiles for base-camp defense.

It was a sizable force, but as deep as they were going into Han-held territory, Rosemont would have liked to stack the deck a little more in his favor. He would have preferred to bring along a section or two of Hulks with his company, as well, but they were all tied up keeping an eye on the TASA Toro suits bottled up in the valley. And since it had not been reported that the Han had powered-suit infantry, this would be a pure grunt-to-grunt affair.

This would be a classic air mobile operation, the perfect employment of his light infantry company. The Hook Talon gunships would clear the landing zones while the grunt platoons landed. After sweeping their area, they would be picked up and flown to a new LZ to do it again. While this was going on, the recon teams would be ranging far ahead of the grunts in the Bubble Tops scouting new LZs and looking for signs of the hostiles.

When the recon teams finally made contact with the main Han forces, they could try to contain them while the Tac Air gunships and the weapons platoon pounded them flat. If all went as planned, next they would go into a pursuit operation, run down the survivors and completely destroy them as a fighting force.

The battle they had fought in the valley had not been the best use of Rosemont's light infantry platoons. Holding static defensive positions had sacrificed their main strengths of mobility and flexibility. Here these strengths would be exploited to the fullest. With the resources he had on hand for the operation, Echo Company should deal with up to two battalions of Han infantry. Any more than that, however, and he'd have to pull back and scream for help. But from what Delta Company had reported, he should be able to handle it alone.

EVEN THOUGH it was still dark, hitting the first landing zone went as flawlessly as an air mobile exercise back at Fort Benning. The area was clean of hostiles, but the gunships still swarmed protectively over the LZ as the Tilt Wings touched down to off-load Mick Sullivan's First Platoon. The instant they were on the ground, the grunts fanned out and quickly secured the area. As soon as Sullivan flashed him the all-clear signal, Rosemont broke out of orbit and took the rest of the formation on to the next LZ.

Several klicks farther on, Jeb Stuart's Second Platoon was preparing to make their insertion. Suddenly one of the Bubble Tops reported suspicious movement in the valley below the hilltop landing zone. The troop lift ships hurried to an orbit well out of range while the scout ships and a gunship escort swooped down to investigate. When the movement was found to be only a roaming flock of llamas, the all-clear signal was sent. The Tilt Wings quickly returned, dropped down and disgorged their troops.

When Stuart's people had secured their LZ, Rosemont took the remainder of the flight on to his planned CP base camp. Again the LZ was clean, and they touched down immediately on the barren hilltop. Once they were out of the planes, Ashley's recon platoon troops quickly established a perimeter while the small headquarters staff started setting up the company CP.

A clear, cold dawn was just breaking over the high mountain plateau when the second flight of Tilt Wings bringing in the weapons platoon and the Thunderbolts appeared. By then, Top Ravenstein had the command post in operation. The comlinks with headquarters and the platoons had been established, and the tactical computers were up and running. Most importantly, however, the first sergeant had his powercell coffeepot going, and the smell of the hot brew was strong on the chill mountain air.

While the Thunderbolt launcher and its radars were being set up, Rivera supervised the offloading of one of his rocket mortar firing sections and their support equipment. That section would stay to protect the CP, and Rosemont was sending the other section out to establish a firebase that could support the two grunt platoons' forward positions.

When he received the message that the firebase had been established, Echo Company was ready to go to work. The first thing Rosemont did was send the recon teams out to scout up some business for them.

THIS WAS sure one hell of a weird country, Ironstone thought as he shivered in the high-altitude cold and pulled his cammo jacket tighter around him. The morning sun was shining brightly, but it gave no warmth. First he had been boiling in the jungle, now he was freezing his nuts off on a barren mountain plateau and he was still in Brazil. Like all professional soldiers, he wondered why wars were never fought in moderate climates. Someplace like southern California or Florida would be a nice change.

As soon as Echo Company had finished taking up their positions, Rosemont had sent Ashley's recon teams out to scout the area before he decided on what his next move would be. As always, Strider Alpha was well out in front. Immediately after their insertion, Kat had led her team deep into the foothills on the western side of this high mountain plateau. The terrain was as barren and forbidding as it was rugged, but it was good terrain for mountain troops, and it looked as if Ironstone had found some. A ten-man patrol was slowly making its way toward him.

Through the imagers in his visor, he could make out the approaching hostiles, wearing what appeared to be dark tan quilted jackets and pants. The Han might not be as technically sophisticated as the Peacekeepers, but they seemed to be one hell of a lot warmer. He decided that the first chance he got, he was going to scrag himself a Han jacket, cut it into a vest and wear it under his chameleon cammos as long as he was in these mountains.

It looked as if he was going to get that chance at a warm quilted jacket real soon. If the Han kept on moving the way they were, the patrol would be in range within fifteen minutes. He quickly flashed the data to Kat on his comlink and powered up his laser ranging scope.

One of the few positive things about being in the mountains was that he could use his sniper rifle to its best advantage up here. The Brazilian jungles were 5 mm LAR country, but the long-range, 8 mm M-41 SASR came into its own in barren landscape like this. With its variable-power scope, he could reach out and touch someone at a klick and a half, nine times out of ten.

While Kat quickly put the rest of the team in supporting positions, Ironstone watched through his scope as the patrol leader led the way along the narrow mountain track. Though the Han patrol was still a thousand meters away, it was time to start the party before they got too much closer.

Carefully focusing the sniper rifle's ranging scope on the officer's chest, the Indian sniper took up the slack on the trigger and, deeply inhaling, filled his chest with the thin, cold mountain air. Slowly letting his breath out, he gently squeezed the trigger, and the silenced rifle spat.

A thousand meters away, the officer jerked with the impact of the 8 mm round and slowly crumpled to the ground. One of his men bent over him to see what had happened. When he saw the blood, he straightened up abruptly, shouted to his comrades and, unslinging his Type 98 assault rifle, looked around the rocks in front of them.

Ironstone's second shot took him in the head.

Now the patrol knew what was happening and dived for cover in the rocks along the trail. Before they could all get out of sight, Ironstone had killed one more and wounded another. Three and a half out of ten wasn't bad at this range. Now the odds were about even, six-and-a-half Han against the four-man recon team.

The Han still did not know where their enemies were, and this left them with a disadvantage. A scattering of shots, intended more as a recon by fire than as an effective counterambush move, broke out. Since none of it was coming anywhere near him, Ironstone sat tight, his scope still focused on the rocks along the trail. He knew that if he was patient they would get curious, and curiosity killed more than just the cat.

One Han stuck his head out for a quick look and was rewarded with a bullet through the brain. Now his comrades opened up with a full barrage of fire, burning through their magazines. When their ineffective fire slowly petered out, Ironstone sent another round their way just to remind them that he was still there.

The invisible, silent death was finally too much for the Han to take. Scrambling to their feet, the survivors dropped their weapons and dashed back down the trail as fast as their feet would take them. Even so, Ironstone was able to take out two more before they reached safety around the bend in the trail.

"Not bad for a redskin, Ironman," Kat commented when she joined him.

"Not bad? Not bad?" Ironstone was indignant. "What in the hell are you talking about, woman? That was damn good shooting and you know it."

Kat smirked. "It looks to me like three of them got away from you."

"You think you could have done any better?" he asked.

"Well, I'd have let them get in a little closer where we all could have taken a shot at them. That way we could have gotten them all."

"If you want—" he gestured in the direction of the retreating Han "—you can go after them."

"I just might do exactly that," she said thoughtfully. "I'd like to find out what those guys were doing up here, anyway."

It took nearly twenty minutes for the recon team to reach the ambush site. The first thing they did when they got there was to search the Han bodies for Intel material, but they came up with very little. Next they gathered up the weapons and ammunition into a large pile for destruction before they moved out.

Kat looked up and saw Ironstone roll a corpse over and quickly strip him of his quilted jacket. Her eyes widened when he pulled the fighting knife from the sheath on his boot top. "What in the hell are you doing, Ironman?" she asked. "Taking scalps, now?"

Without bothering to answer, he neatly cut the sleeves from the jacket and dropped them back on the body. Shrugging out of his cammo jacket, he smiled as he donned the quilted vest. "Ah," he said. "It's still warm."

Kat shuddered. "Jesus, Ironstone."

WHEN KAT FLASHED the report of the successful ambush back to the Echo Company CP, Rosemont ordered her to continue the mission. He was holding both of his grunt platoons in their defensive positions until he could get a better fix on the Han forces. Delta Company's Intel was spotty at best, and if there were more hostiles out there than they had reported, his single company might not have enough firepower to handle them by themselves.

The colonel had already given them first priority on the force Tac Air assets and had promised immediate reinforcement if Rosemont needed it. But it was better to know exactly what was out there before he stuck his neck out than to step in it and have to call for help to keep from getting it cut off.

THE NEXT TIME Ironstone spotted the hostiles, the Indian sniper wisely held his fire. There was no way he was going to get into a pissing contest with a full company of elite Han mountain troops. Going to ground in a pile of large boulders on the top of a small hill, he flashed a message back for Kat to come forward.

"What you got, Ironman?" she asked as she slid in beside him.

He pointed to the ridge line across the valley in front of him. At least a reinforced company of Han mountain infantry was occupying well-prepared defensive positions along the top of the ridge. Through her imagers Kat could see that they had infantry mortars with them and other heavy weapons, but she saw no sign of antiaircraft batteries.

"I wonder what in the hell they're doing up there," she muttered to herself as she quickly plotted all the positions she could make out on her tacscreen. "It doesn't look like there's anything around here worth defending with that much firepower."

This part of the Andes was largely barren rolling terrain covered with stunted scrub brush. Her map didn't indicate any towns or mines in the area that would warrant this kind of defense.

"Maybe they're trying to control the approach into the valley down there," Ironstone said.

"But why? What's behind the valley?"

"Why don't we just march on over there and ask them what they're doing? They seem like reasonable fellows to me." Since Ironstone had not been with Kat on her last mission when she and a handful of the headquarters people, including the major, had been shot down in Han territory, he did not have her appreciation of the Han military mentality.

"Your ass, Ironman," Kat hissed. "I had more than enough of those bastards the last time. I'm not getting any closer to those guys until I've got some backup.''

She keyed her mike implant. "Bold Lancer, this is Strider Alpha. Over."

"Lancer, go," Rosemont answered.

"Strider. I found 'em."

"Lancer, flash it."

12

In the Andes—15 November

When he received Kat's comlink message, Rosemont immediately sprang into action. Finally he had something useful for the rest of his people to do, and it was something they should be able to handle without too much outside help. Quickly working out a plan of attack utilizing both his grunt platoons, the weapons platoon and the on-call Tac Air support, he flashed it back to the force ops center. As he expected, Mad Mike immediately signed off on it and told him to go to it.

Rosemont flashed the warning orders to the platoons and signaled for the Tilt Wings to crank up. After the initial early-morning air assaults, four of the assault transports had remained at his CP, one as his C-and-C ship and the other three ships for troop lift. Two Tilt Wings could carry a full grunt platoon, so he could move his troops into position in just two lifts.

The minute Rosemont boarded his C-and-C ship, the aircraft lifted off and headed for Kat's contact. Two of the other Tilt Wings quickly rose from the ground behind him and vectored off to Sullivan's position.

The third aircraft waited, her turbines spooled up and her rotors spinning, while Hank Rivera's gun bunnies quickly broke down their two rocket mortars and loaded them into the ship. When the gunners had the weapons securely tied down, the support people passed crates of rocket ammunition into the aircraft and lashed them down around the disassembled tube. As soon as the last crate was loaded, Rivera and the gun crews clambered on board. The Tilt Wing lifted off in a flurry of dust and headed for the recon contact as fast as her screaming turbines could carry her.

A little over halfway to the target area, Rivera spotted a small hill standing clear of the surrounding terrain. The hill was well within the maximum range for the rocket mortars, it was easily defendable, and there were no hostiles anywhere in the area. It was a perfect firebase. "Down there," he told the pilot.

Before the aircraft's rotors had even stopped turning, the gunners had the rear ramp door down and were rapidly unloading the mortars and ammunition. While the gun crews quickly assembled their weapons and loaded the ammo feed trays with the 120 mm rocket projectiles, Rivera set up the FDC monitor and linked it to the main fire computer in Rosemont's C-and-C ship.

"We're up," the gun captain told Rivera.

"Bold Lancer," Rivera said to Rosemont. "Bold Thunder Xray. We're in position, locked and loaded."

"Lancer, affirm," Rosemont answered. "Flashing targets now."

The DFC monitor screen lit up with the ten mortar fire concentrations Rosemont had plotted to support the attack on the Han position.

"Thunder Xray, confirm Ficon one through ten."

"Lancer, affirm. Fire by number on my command."

"Thunder Xray, standing by."

ROSEMONT'S C-AND-C SHIP was orbiting well out of range of the Han position when the two Tilt Wings carrying Sullivan's First Platoon caught up with him. "Bold Lancer, Bold Racer," Mick called. "We're on station."

"Lancer affirm," Rosemont answered. "Taclink with Strider Alpha for your Lima Zulu."

"Racer, affirm."

Keeping to nap of the earth, Sullivan's two Tilt Wings stayed well down out of sight as they flew in behind the ridge line and flared out for a landing on the flat behind Strider Alpha's position. Sullivan's people quickly off-loaded and took their position on the reverse slope of the ridge. If Rosemont's plan went as he expected, they would have a ringside seat for the battle from the ridge line. If there were any problems, they would be sent in to reinforce Stuart's Second Platoon.

As soon as the Tilt Wings dropped off Sullivan's people, they lifted off to pick up Stuart's Second Platoon, the ground-assault force for the operation. As soon as the weapons platoon had blasted the Han positions, Jeb's grunts would go in and take the ground the old-fashioned way: they would fight for it.

Less than twenty minutes later, Stuart's Second Platoon grunts were on station with their Tilt Wings orbiting well out of sight with Rosemont's C-and-C ship. After they arrived, there was another brief wait until the Tac Air gunship reinforcements Rosemont had requested could arrive from force headquarters.

"Bold Lancer, Hook Talon Lead," the Tac Air flight leader called.

"Lancer, go."

"Talon Lead. I'm ETA zero-two with three guns and a pair of Dustoffs. We're ready to go to work."

"Lancer affirm, stand by for taclink."

"Talon, send it."

Rosemont flashed the data for the hostile positions, the fire-support plan and the ground assault.

"Talon, good copy," the flight leader acknowledged. "We'll orbit off to the north. Go get 'em, Lancer."

After checking one last time to make sure that everyone was in place and ready, he keyed his mike implant. "Bold Thunder Xray, this is Bold Lancer. Ficon one, three, four, six and eight. Battery four, fire!"

AT ROSEMONT'S COMMAND, the mortar gunners tripped their firing pedals, and the first two 120 mm rocket rounds left the tubes with a whoosh, trailing dirty white smoke from their rocket motors. In seconds they were followed by two more as the mortars

cycled rounds from the feed trays. The ammo humpers stood by the trays, keeping them full of the heavy
multipurpose projectiles.

After both tubes had fired four rounds at the first
Ficon in under a minute, they automatically shifted
fire to the next target. The FDC computer fed the data
to the guns to aim them, and all the gunners had to do
was to keep the feed trays loaded.

The computer also controlled the detonation of the
120 mm warheads. The rounds that fell on the Han
infantry positions burst high in the air and rained
shrapnel down upon their unprotected heads. The
rocket warheads that were targeted against the Han
vehicles and weapons positions, however, were programmed to wait until they hit their targets before
detonating.

The effect of the sudden barrage was devastating.
The weapons platoon called their rocket mortar fire
high-angle hell, and hell was certainly walking through
the Han's positions today. One minute the Han had
been all alone in their remote hilltop, and the next
minute, EHE death was raining down upon them.

The troops caught out in the open died as they raced
for cover. Those in their trenches and bunkers did not
fare that much better. Their overhead cover protected
them from the antipersonnel rounds, but not all the
rounds exploded in the air. Some of the rocket salvos
were of mixed concentrations. The first rounds burst
in the air to sweep those Han caught out in the open.
The succeeding rounds were fuzed to detonate on

contact and dig them out of their bunkers and trenches.

Rosemont watched the barrage on his tac monitor and, when the last rounds were in the air, flashed the assault order to the waiting Tilt Wings and gunships.

Before the smoke even had a chance to clear, the Bubble Tops and gunships were swooping down from the clear sky, blasting the Han positions that had escaped the deadly mortar barrage. Covered by the devastating fire of the 20 mm chain guns of the Bubble Tops and the gunships, Stuart's grunts made their assault.

The Tilt Wings screamed in fast and low to the ground as they approached the hill. At the last possible moment, their rotors went into full reverse pitch and their wings pivoted to brake their forward speed. Skidding to a halt in a barely controlled crash, the assault transports had their rear ramp doors down and locked before their wheels even touched the ground.

Screaming their war cries, Stuart's grunts raced out of the aircraft. Splitting up into assault teams, they charged the trenches, their LARs and grenade launchers blazing fire. Although they were stunned by the rocket mortar attack, the Han regrouped and valiantly tried to defend their hilltop. Fierce firefights broke out as the grunts closed with them.

Orbiting off to the side in his C-and-C ship, Rosemont was able to follow the progress of the battle on his tac monitors better than if he was actually in the middle of it. The computers showed the location beacons of the Peacekeepers and filtered the hostiles' po-

sitions from the jumble of input from the grunts'
helmet sensors and imagers into a coherent mosaic of
blue-and-red markers on the screen. The only way he
could have had a better picture of the battle would be
from inside a hovering Bubble Top, directly overhead
the area.

He watched closely as the assault teams worked to
clear the Han trenches and bunkers. One by one the
markers on the monitor indicating the hostile positions turned from red to blue. Occasionally a Peacekeeper's marker changed from blue to blinking yellow,
indicating that he or she had been wounded. Surpris-
ingly, though, there were few casualty markers.

When the Han on the western side of the hill tried
to mount a counterattack, Rosemont was able to spot
their buildup in time. Flashing Rivera's mortars to fire
another barrage, he sent airburst rocket mortar rounds
down to break them up. When the counterattack was
blasted, the half-dozen skimmers that had survived the
attack immediately cranked up and made a run for it
down the hill.

Rosemont had wisely left the Han an open avenue
of retreat leading out of their position to the west. To
completely bottle them up would only make them fight
that much harder and would cost him even more casualties. Also, since he was looking for their main
forces, he was hoping that the survivors of this attack
would lead him to them.

When he saw the gunships wheel around to go after
the fleeing vehicles, Rosemont called to the gunship
flight leader. "Hook Talon Lead, Bold Lancer."

"Talon, go."

"Lancer. Don't make it too difficult for them to get away. We need to follow them to their nest."

"Talon affirm," the gunship flight leader answered in an amused tone of voice. "We'll let some of them get away for you."

As Rosemont watched, Talon Lead lined up on the last skimmer in the fleeing column and blew it into a dozen flaming pieces with a Long Lash missile. Then, after a moment's hesitation, he sharply pulled off of his gun run as if he was out of ammunition and let the other vehicles escape.

WHEN STUART FLASHED that the hostile position had been secured, Rosemont directed his pilot to set down in the center of the hilltop. Jeb Stuart was waiting to meet him when he stepped off the plane. The platoon leader was dirty and smoke stained and he had a patch of drying blood in the right sleeve of his chameleon suit. But the smile on his face told Rosemont that the blood wasn't his.

"One hilltop ready for your inspection, sir," Stuart reported, his eyes glittering with adrenaline.

"Good work, Jeb," Rosemont answered. "What were your casualties?"

"Not that bad," the platoon leader answered as he called up the butcher's bill on his helmet visor. "Only one dead and eight wounded."

Rosemont looked around, noting the number of Han fortifications that had been neutralized by Rivera's artillery barrage or the Hook Talon gunships. "That's not too bad, Jeb, considering."

The lieutenant followed Rosemont's eyes, mentally counting the large number of hostile corpses lying in the wreckage of their bunkers and trenches. "Yeah, Hank's boys did a real good job this time. They saved us a lot of heartache. I need to buy them all a beer when we get back to Benning."

"Speaking of beer," Rosemont said, "tell your people that the first one's on me when we stand down. Also make sure that you give me your recommendations for awards."

"That's most affirm, sir."

The platoon medics were already treating the wounded, both Peacekeeper and Han alike. Treatment priority went to the grunts, of course, but the hostile casualties were also looked after. The Peacekeepers didn't hold grudges, and once the battle was over and their enemies had been defeated, they were treated with the same concern as anyone else. The only difference was that once they received medical attention, they were put in with the rest of the POWs.

Along with the wounded Han, several of them had been captured unhurt. They were all being thoroughly searched and having their hands cuffed behind them to await transport back to force headquarters, where they would be interrogated. If Rosemont couldn't track down the main concentration of the Han forces, running the POWs through the interrogation process would reveal it.

While the grunts finished securing the battlefield and searched through the smashed wreckage of the men and the bunkers, Rosemont flashed a quick report of his success back to the force ops center.

NOW THAT THE HAN had finally been located, the force commander authorized hot pursuit as they fled back into Peru. Observing the niceties of national boundaries took second place to getting the situation in western Brazil firmly under control once and for all. In fact, the colonel was so concerned about it that he had authorized a "rampage" mission.

A "rampage" was an all-out operation allowing the Peacekeepers to range far and wide to search out and destroy the enemy wherever found. Once the Peacekeepers had been loosed to do what they did best, they would not stop until the last hostile was facedown in the sand with a boot on the back of his neck.

The term "rampage" had first been applied to describe USEF search-and-destroy operations by a young reporter from the *New Berkeley Voice,* the last of the old ultraliberal newsfaxes in the United States. The reporter's liberal sensibilities had been aroused to a fever pitch when he had toured a combat zone in Pakistan after the Peacekeepers had gone through, successfully eliminating the serious Pakistani nuclear-weapons threat to peace in the region.

It was true that the area was a mess as only a war-ravaged land could be. The Pakistani troops had fought hard to save their outlawed nukes, and the Peacekeepers had fought even harder. The crops were torn up by vehicles and blasted by artillery, as always happened in a combat zone. Bodies lay in the streets and fields where they had fallen, but they had all been the bodies of combatants, not women and children. The facilities and buildings that had been destroyed had all had military significance.

The excessively idealistic reporter had chosen only to see the horrors of war, the death and the destruction. He had not wanted to see that the nuclear weapons that had threatened India and the Middle East had been rendered into so much radioactive scrap by the USEF. He had hysterically used the word "rampage" in his completely biased reports to describe the Peacekeepers' campaign, hoping to arouse a storm of protest from the far Left. But his smear campaign failed. Instead, the entire world had praised their efforts to make the planet a safer place to live, and the word had been adopted by the USEF as a term of pride.

This would be a minirampage, however, as the entire force wasn't taking part in it. Even a minirampage was an all-out operation and it would not end until the Han were no longer a threat to western Brazil.

13

In the Andes—15 November

While one of the Bubble Top scout ships shadowed the
rapidly retreating Han, Rosemont's grunts quickly resupplied and regrouped to continue their attack. As
soon as the casualties had been treated, they were
loaded into the waiting MH-39 Dustoff Medevac
choppers and flown back to the force field hospital.
Fortunately, though, there were few serious friendly
casualties and only the one death. The overwhelming
mortar fire support and sudden aerial assault had once
more proven the old military maxim that the best defense was a strong offense.

Rosemont left Hank Rivera's weapons platoon
broken down into the two firing sections for the pursuit operation that would follow next. That way they
could leapfrog one another to keep up with the advancing grunts and provide them with an umbrella of
constant on-call fire support if the Han stopped and
turned to fight.

When the Bat UAVs and their mother ship arrived
on station, the Bubble Top pulled away from the fleeing Han and left the tracking to the UAVs as it re-

turned to refuel. Rather than send the aircraft back to force headquarters for fuel, Rosemont requested two Bladder Birds to save time. Working in relays, the Tilt Wings, Bubble Tops and Hook Talon gunships were topped off with fuel, rearmed and made ready to continue the mission.

Less than an hour later, Sullivan's First Platoon and a gunship escort was back in the air racing after the Han.

ROSEMONT HAD half expected the Han to stop and turn to fight, but they didn't. They continued their headlong flight until they reached an area outside a small town situated on a high mountain plateau. Back in his C-and-C ship, Rosemont monitored the pursuit carefully as Sullivan shadowed them safely out of range of antiaircraft missiles.

"Lancer, Bold Racer, I think we've got them," Sullivan reported from his Tilt Wing. "They've stopped just this side of a little place called Madre de Dios."

"Lancer. What did you say that name was?"

"Madre de Dios."

"That means Mother of God, doesn't it?"

"That's affirm, Lancer." Sullivan was one of the company's Spanish linguists. "It's a strange name for a town, but that's what's on the map."

"What does it look like they're doing?"

"According to what I'm getting here, Lancer, they're pulling in at some kind of a compound out in the middle of nowhere—it could be military. And your plan worked, we flushed them out. They're being joined by a mechanized infantry column moving in from the northwest. I'm reading at least a battalion down there, and they're digging in, but I'm not getting much in the line of heavy-weapons readings. Flashing target data up-link now."

"Lancer, good copy," Rosemont sent back when he saw the hostile data appear on his tac monitor. "Keep out of range, we'll be there ASAP. Be prepared to go into a ground assault on order."

"Racer, affirm. We'll be ready."

Rosemont quickly flashed target data and orders to the other Tilt Wings and gunships accompanying him. Now that the Han had been run to ground, it was time to go in and destroy them.

THE FIGHT WAS A RERUN of the battle for the hilltop earlier that day. Again Hank Rivera's rocket mortars rained their deadly 120 mm projectiles down onto the Han positions. They were even more effective this time because the hostiles had not had time to dig in and protect themselves from the high-angle fire.

After a sustained mortar barrage from both of Rivera's firing sections, Rosemont landed both of his grunt platoons and the recon teams. As before, the recon teams occupied blocking positions while the grunt platoons did what they had been designed to do: close with and destroy the enemy.

Even with the two platoons moving in on them from the ground while Rivera's weapons platoon pounded them from the air, the Han fought furiously. They were taking tremendous casualties, but it didn't slow them down. Rather than surrender, the Han continued fighting as they withdrew from their forward positions, pulling their perimeter in tight around the compound.

The stubborn Han defense of the small facility puzzled Rosemont. From what he could see, it didn't look like a military compound. There were no stacked supplies, motor pool or other marks of a military installation. It looked more like a factory of some kind with the one main building and a couple of smaller structures inside a fence. Or, it suddenly dawned on him, maybe it was a laboratory.

"All Lancer elements," he sent over the comlink. "This is Bold Lancer. Do not, I say again, do not fire on the main building in the compound. I want it taken intact."

"Bold Racer," Sullivan sent back. "Be advised that some of them are holed up in there, using it for cover."

"Take 'em out with snipers. I do not want that building damaged by heavy fire."

"Racer, affirm."

RATHER THAN TAKE unacceptable casualties, Rosemont had ordered the grunts to back off and called in more mortar fire. A sustained pounding ended the battle when the remnants of the Han finally surrendered.

With the last of the Han out of action, Rosemont landed his C-and-C ship on the chopper landing pad right outside the fenced compound and stepped out.

When Jeb met him this time, the blood on his uniform was his own. "You're hit," Rosemont said.

Stuart shrugged. "A piece of frag, sir. I can't even feel it yet."

"Give me your platoon sergeant and get that attended to ASAP."

"Yes, sir."

Outside the compound fence, the medics were treating the casualties, and the grunts were rounding up those few Han who had surrendered. Some of the POWs were not wearing Han military uniforms, but were dressed in white clothing that looked suspiciously like lab jackets or sterile suits.

Curious as to what was in the compound the Han had fought so hard to keep, Rosemont himself went to investigate. The main building bore scars of small-arms fire and shell fragments in the roof and walls, but it was mostly intact. A single glance through the building's main door showed Rosemont all he needed to see.

There was some kind of lab set up inside with clean rooms, culture tanks and meters upon meters of glass and stainless-steel fixtures. It could be nothing except the biological-warfare lab he was looking for.

A shiver ran through him when he realized what he was looking at and what it represented. He pulled away from the door frame as if he feared being contaminated even though he knew that he had been protected by the immunization.

"All Lancer elements, this is Bold Lancer," Rosemont sent out over the comlink. "Pull everyone back

ASAP. I want them at least a klick away and upwind from this compound at all times. Keep this place under close observation, but no one's to go in here without my express permission. And no one is to take anything from that building or this compound, nothing at all. Absolutely no souvenirs this time. Acknowledge in turn."

"Bold Racer, affirm," Sullivan sent. "Is it the lab?"

"Lancer, that's most affirm."

"Bold Cowboy, acknowledged."

"Bold Strider," Ashley sent. "We're moving now."

"Hook Talon," the flight leader transmitted. "We're outta here."

THE DISCOVERY of the Han biological-warfare laboratory in Peru instantly became the most important item of the entire South American agenda. The Han government, of course, denied any knowledge of the laboratory. They also denied that any of their troops were deployed in Peru. They did admit, however, that many of the Han who had emigrated to Peru had become citizens of that nation and that some of them may have volunteered to go into the Peruvian armed forces.

That explanation did not account for the fact that no Peruvian officers had been killed or captured with the units or that the latest Han-issue military equipment and uniforms had been found on the captives. But it served to get the Han government off the hook on that account. International politics has always been built on face-saving half truths, and no one had expected anything different this time. Nonetheless, there was still the matter of the clandestine laboratory, and the Han couldn't deny that it existed.

Germ warfare was so indiscriminately destructive that it was even more feared than mere nuclear devastation. Nuclear-weapons effects could be anticipated and, while destructive, they were limited by the laws of physics. Biological weapons, on the other hand, were completely uncontrollable. Once they were released, they were carried on the air and in the water and infected everyone who came in contact with them. Also, unlike a nuke detonation, they continued killing men, women and children indiscriminately. If biological weapons were being used, all of South America faced a dire threat.

While Echo Company guarded the remote laboratory facility, the International Red Cross and UN medical teams quickly flew in to confirm that the lab was in fact what it appeared to be. As Rosemont had surmised, it was a biological-warfare laboratory.

When Rosemont's suspicions had been confirmed, he requested and immediately received permission to pull his people well back and employ sensors to keep an eye on the place.

The strictest precautions were called for to prevent further spread of the deadly virus. Not only had most of the grunts in Delta Company fallen victim to the deadly mutated flu virus, but it had begun to appear in the civilian population as well. So far, most of the new victims were in remote Peruvian mountain communities in the vicinity of the lab, but an outbreak of the mutated flu had been reported inside western Brazil. United Nations vaccination teams were immediately dispatched to the infected areas, but for many it was too late.

After lengthy consultations with both the American government and the United Nations, the force commander made the final decision to employ the ultimate measure to contain the biological threat.

Two DAYS AFTER the laboratory had been discovered, only a lone recon team guarded the complex and they were in hardened bunker positions twenty-five kilometers away. Everyone else, including the entire population of Madre de Dios, both humans and animals, had been evacuated from the high plateau from a radius of a hundred kilometers around the lab.

Right at twelve o'clock noon, the harsh light of the mountain sun faded in the glare from a man-made sun that suddenly appeared in the sky high above the Han laboratory complex. The glare came from a kilo of gaseous tritium that had been heated hotter than the sun in an instant by a small nuclear explosion. Hydrogen nuclei in the superheated tritium grudgingly gave up their electrons and reformed into helium molecules. In the process, they gave off energy in accordance with the Einsteinian formula $E = mc^2$, the nuclear equation.

In an instant the Han laboratory and everything around it for a kilometer ceased to exist except as scattered, glowing molecules blown on the superheated wind. In that same instant, all life in the area, even the mutated virus, ceased to exist in the sterilizing nuclear fire.

The thunderclap of the detonation echoed from the faraway mountain peaks. Startled, the nesting Andean condors took to the air with strong beats of their massive wings. Mere feathered wings of bone, muscle and sinew could not prevail this time, and the majestic birds were immediately blown out of the sky by the shock wave of the nuclear blast.

A dreaded mushroom-shaped cloud slowly formed over the small lake of glowing molten glass that had once been the Han compound. The cap of the mushroom cloud boiled with a riot of colors as superheated molecules were sucked up into it, stripped of their electrons and broken up into subatomic particles.

Even in their hardened positions kilometers away, the Peacekeepers flinched and pressed themselves closer to the ground. They had all been through the nuke-weapons training in the cyber tanks, but a primitive fear overcame their training. This was the real thing, not a cyberspace computer simulation, and even the bravest shrank from the awesome power of a nuclear detonation.

As soon as the mushroom cloud had dissipated in the high-altitude winds, a lone UAV-15C Bat recon vehicle flew over the lab site. The aerial recon vehicle circled the glowing crater, its sensors recording the devastation below. As soon as the mission was over and the data had been flashed to the UAV controllers, the Bat was vectored far out over the Pacific Ocean.

When it was above the two-kilometer-deep Peruvian Trench, the Bat nosed over and dived straight for the water below. For the remainder of eternity, the radioactive aerial vehicle would safely rest on the floor of the Pacific Ocean, where it would not pose the danger of contaminating life on earth.

WHEN THE TILT WINGS arrived to pick up the recon team observers, the men and women were subdued. They talked only in hushed tones and moved slowly as if they were tired. It was an exhaustion of the spirit, not of the body, that affected them. While their mission had been successful in removing the threat of the mutated virus, they felt that somehow they had failed.

The primary mission of the Peacekeepers was to protect the planet from nuclear destruction. In order to protect it from something just as bad, if not worse, they had been forced to detonate a nuke weapon themselves. Now that they had let the nuclear genie out of the bottle, they feared what would come after it.

14

The United Nations—21 November

The first detonation of a nuclear weapon since the one-day Arab-Israeli War of 1994 shocked the world into stunned silence. Even the argumentative delegates in the chambers of the United Nations were speechless for a welcome change. The shock was short-lived, however, and the diplomatic shouting and yelling soon began anew. As they had done from the beginning of this conflict, the Greens were screaming the loudest of all.

This time, however, the Greens were divided right down the middle. Some of them automatically decried the use of the nuclear sterilizing strike. It didn't matter that it had probably saved South America from a serious plague that could have killed millions. A nuke was a nuke, no matter how it had been used, and they were totally opposed to anything nuclear. Their followers attacked nuclear power plants, throwing themselves bodily against the electrified fences and the guard dogs. The body count was substantial.

The other contingent of Greens raged about the rampant evils of the genetic-engineering technology that had made the manufacture of the mutated virus possible. They called for an immediate search of the entire planet for other secret bioengineering labs and called for them to be immediately nuked, as well. Their followers raided medical-research facilities, destroying millions of dollars' worth of equipment and thousands of experiments. Since they attacked mostly at night, they lost few people.

Other politicians, not generally known for their support of the Green platform, quickly got in on this argument. A woman senator from California stood up in Congress and delivered her proposal for a bill that would prohibit all genetic-engineering technology in the United States. Another senator, a man whose children suffered from a genetic disorder that was eased by treatment with a bioengineered enzyme, immediately denounced her as being a hysterical Luddite.

She countered by filing a sexual-discrimination suit against him for his having called her hysterical. The judge allowed the suit to proceed because the word *hysterical* was derived from the ancient Greek word for uterus and thereby was de facto discriminatory against all women.

For a brief moment, no one argued about the TASA-Brazilian war. The illegal logging site and the massacre of the UN Green Police that had started the war had been completely forgotten. In fact, the ceremonial funeral of the fallen UN Green Police officers didn't even make the evening newscasts that night.

Slotted in its place was a panel discussion about female hormonal disorders and rational thinking.

WITH THE DESTRUCTION of the Han forces in Peru, the defense of the western border of their nation was now turned over to the Brazilians. The Brazilian army had fully recovered from the earlier debacle and was fit for combat duty. An emergency military-aid bill had been pushed through the American Congress, and they were being reequipped with modern infantry tank-killing weapons and light tactical aircraft. After the selected Brazilian units had been reequipped and trained to use the new equipment, they were sent out in case more Han "volunteers" appeared.

Once the Brazilians were in place, Rosemont and Echo Company returned to their positions in the Passo Fundo Valley. In their absence, a couple of minor skirmishes had been fought, but the front lines had remained almost the same. So had the TASA forces arrayed against them. The battles that had been fought in the small valley had only been the opening acts of the real battle waiting to be fought.

As soon as Echo Company had settled back into their old positions, the force commander called an officers' meeting. When all the other routine business had been concluded, the force commander, Colonel Jacobson, took the podium.

"First off," he said, "I'd like to welcome Major Rosemont back and say 'job very well done.'"

Rosemont smiled and nodded to accept the compliment.

"Also," the colonel continued, "I would like to report that Delta Company has recovered from their bout with the flu and will be coming back on-line tomorrow."

That brought a round of applause from everyone in the room. The Delta Devils had been missed.

"Now for the general situation," Jacobson said as he flashed a map up on the large holoscreen at the front of the room showing the current disposition of forces. "First, you might be interested to know that the Argies have been able to stick to their claim that they knew nothing about the Han virus laboratory. And—" he shook his head "—apparently they are being believed.

"And as you know, the combat has now been removed from the battlefield and has been transported to the corridors of power. This, of course, means that we are facing a war of attrition here. Now that the Argies know what we can do to them, they probably won't try to go head-to-head with us again. But the way they figure, time is on their side and they can afford to wait.

"They know that the international community is badly divided on this conflict. It has escalated from a mere ecological and territorial dispute to the use of biological warfare and nuclear weapons. They're betting that the UN will get panicked and order us to pull out and leave the Brazilians to their fate. All we can do to counter this is to hold tight, wait for their next move and be ready to deal with it no matter where it comes from."

Jacobson paused and looked around at the men and women in the room. "I will tell you this, though. The Peacekeepers are here and we are going to do what we came here to do. One way or the other, peace will be restored to this region. And we will not go home until it is."

In the rear of the tent, someone started the chant, "War! War! War!"

Colonel Jacobson could not prevent a faint smile from crossing his lips as the chanting grew louder.

When the force sergeant major dismissed the briefing, he had to shout to be heard.

To KEEP his people's minds on the business of war, Rosemont made sure they had plenty of work to do. As with all professional military units, boredom could be a real killer on the battlefield.

To keep the grunts on their toes, he even borrowed a section of Hulks and used them to run training exercises in combating powered fighting suits in anticipation of going against the TASA Toro suits again. When the grunts weren't training, they were cleaning their weapons and pulling maintenance on their equipment.

That didn't mean that there wasn't time left to relax and enjoy November in the Brazilian countryside. Since they were in the Southern Hemisphere, the weather was springlike and not too hot. Rosemont also knew the value of time off and, in between training and maintenance, he saw that everyone got some slack time.

Spike Salazar was also going out of his way to see that the grunts of Echo Company enjoyed their stay. One day he brought in the Brazilian gaucho equivalent of a Wild West rodeo to Echo Company's area for their entertainment.

That was when Rosemont learned that Ashley was an accomplished horsewoman. One of the gauchos saw her examining his horse, a magnificent stallion, and he asked her in Spanish if she rode. Flashing the cowboy a bright smile, she vaulted onto the saddle and proceeded to put on a brilliant display of trick riding.

"I didn't know you could ride," Rosemont said when she brought the horse back to the applause of the gauchos.

She slid off the saddle with a big smile on her face. "There's a lot about me you don't know," she said. "I had my own pony when I was five. I played polo when I was in high school, and Father always had a racing stable."

"I'm impressed." Rosemont grinned. "Maybe you can teach me to be a better rider tonight."

She smiled slowly. "All it takes is practice."

"That's what I'm hoping."

KAT AND IRONSTONE also enjoyed watching the gauchos put their horses through their paces. "This is your kind of life-style isn't it, Ironman?" Kat asked. "Noble horse warriors of the open plains? Back in the days when men were men and smelled like horses?"

Grinning broadly, Ironstone raised his arm and ducked his nose into his armpit. "I thought I always smelled like a horse."

"Now that you mention it," Kat replied, "I have been meaning to say something to you about that little problem for some time. We do have a shower set up now."

"But I haven't been able to talk you into scrubbing my back yet."

Kat laughed. "Only in your dreams, Ironman."

A young gaucho swaggered up to Kat and Ironstone and said something in rapid-fire Spanish. Ironstone answered in equally fluent Spanish and nodded to Kat.

"What'd he say?" Kat asked.

The Indian glanced down at the teflon fighting knife in her boot-top sheath. "He asked if you knew how to use that knife or if it was merely a macho decoration. I told him that you could use it well enough."

Kat smiled slowly at the young cowboy, her green eyes narrowing. This was her kind of question. "Ask him if he needs a shave."

The young gaucho laughed when Ironstone translated her reply and rattled off an answer.

"He says that he hasn't met a lady barber yet who could shave him."

"You tell him that this sergeant isn't a lady and that I've shaved better men than him."

"He asks if the sergeant would care to engage in a test of skills."

"Sure." Kat laughed. "I'd be glad to teach this kid a thing or two about knife work. Exactly what does he have in mind?"

By now a crowd of gauchos had gathered, drawn by the prospect of some unscheduled entertainment, and they cheered the young man on as he drew his blade. The gaucho's knife was a narrow, double-edged dagger about ten inches long with a fancy silver hilt. It was a good design, but nothing special. "He says a target contest," Ironstone translated.

Kat's hand flashed down to her sheath, and she drew her knife. Though drab, Kat's teflon fighting blade was the result of many years of searching for the ultimate combat knife. "Tell him he's on."

A playing card was quickly stuck in a bale of hay that had been brought for the horses. Backing away ten paces, the gaucho sheathed his knife behind his back and stood crouched with his hands at his side. When one of the watchers shouted "go," he drew the knife and threw. His knife hit the upper right-hand quarter of the card, the ace of spades, and went half way into the bale.

"Not bad," Kat said as she sheathed her knife in her boot top and backed up another five paces. "But you missed the target."

Her hand was a blur as she drew her blade and threw. The gaucho looked and saw Kat's knife buried to the hilt in the exact center of the ace of spades. He smiled confidently. "You are pretty good against targets, Sergeant. But how are you when you go up against a man?"

Kat smiled and looked around slowly. "I can hold my own against a man, but I don't see any men here today."

The gaucho audience hooted and cheered, and Kat's opponent fought to keep from blushing. "I am a man!" he said hotly. "And I can prove it to you, Sergeant. Face me if you dare!"

"To keep this from getting out of hand," Kat told Ironstone, "tell this kid that I'll take him on barehanded. First blood or a disarm."

"He'll cut you, Kat," Ironstone said. "His buddies have been teasing him and he won't back off."

"He'll try," she said. "But he can't really hurt me. I'm wearing my inserts. I'll just take it away from him and end this bullshit."

"Okay," Ironstone replied. "But I think this has gone a little too far."

"It'll be over soon enough." Kat's eyes glittered; she was having fun.

The spectators formed a circle around the two fighters. The young gaucho stood sideways, his knife hand held low in street-fighter style and his off hand held protectively in front of his chest. Kat faced him squarely, her feet well apart and her arms down at her sides.

With no warning, the gaucho lunged, his knife slashing for her midsection. Kat danced away from the blade and backed up, waiting to see what he was going to do next.

The gaucho paused, tossing his knife from hand to hand, another cheap street fighter's trick. But Kat didn't watch the knife; she watched the man's eyes. When she saw his pupils constrict slightly, she launched herself at him. Catching his knife hand, she pivoted on her feet, locking his knife arm safely against her side. Applying a thumb press against his wrist, she instantly disarmed him.

The audience burst out in applause. They were all knife fighters, but they had never seen a real knife-fighting expert in action before. When Kat turned to acknowledge their accolades, the young gaucho snatched up the knife and sprang at her.

"Kat!" Ironstone shouted.

Spinning around, she managed to deflect the blade with her right hand, making it brush past her neck. Her left hand came down in a chop against his upper arm. The sound of his arm snapping was clearly heard.

Kat stepped back, scooped up the knife that had dropped from the gaucho's nerveless fingers and handed it to Ironstone. "See," she said, panting, "I'm not even breathing heavily."

"You are bleeding, though," Ironstone said. "He got you right under the ear."

She dabbed at the small cut. "Little bastard," she growled when she saw the blood. "I ought to really kick his ass for that."

The young gaucho was being tended to by his comrades when an older man broke away and walked over to Kat and bowed his head. *"Señorita,"* he said in heavily accented English. "I hope you are not hurt."

"I'm fine," she said. "How about him?"

The old man shrugged. "His arm, she is broken, but it will heal."

"I'm sorry, but I had no choice."

"Some of our young men," the man said, "they do not have good manners. As soon as his arm is whole again, I will see that he learns the proper respect for a lady."

Kat laughed. "Don't be too hard on him, *señor*. I think he's learned his lesson. Just make sure he doesn't try that with a Peacekeeper again. Some of us would have killed him for that."

The old man looked at her with respect in his eyes. "Thank you for not killing him, *señorita*. He is my worthless son."

Kat raised one eyebrow. "Then I, too, am happy that he will recover. Maybe someday he will be half the man his father is."

The old man bowed again, "I thank you once more, from my heart, *señorita*."

"*De nada.*"

15

Brasilia, Brazil—22 November

Though the war was not raging, the Brazilian people were not reassured that the crisis had passed. In the period of only a few weeks, their nation had been brutally invaded, their army had been humiliated and the hated traditional enemies now occupied a large part of their country. What was even worse, though, was that instead of wanting to come to their assistance, most of the world felt that they deserved to be punished.

The Brazilians had welcomed the USEF as their only hope to keep from being conquered. But now the same nations that had condemned the Brazilians were preventing the Peacekeepers from doing their job and freeing their occupied territories.

This was difficult for a proud people to bear. The worst thing of all had been the discovery that their enemies had attempted to unleash a deadly disease upon their population. The TASA armies, with their Toro suits and armored vehicles, they could fight and, even if they lost, they would go down fighting. But no one could fight an army of deadly engineered viruses.

Brazilian valor, courage and force of arms counted for nothing against these invisible enemies.

Even though the laboratory had been destroyed and the UN medical teams were containing the outbreak of the deadly flu, the Brazilian people feared what would come next. As far as they were concerned, they were truly alone with no hope in sight.

DEEP IN THE WAR ROOM of the capital city of Brasilia, a difficult decision was made only after much discussion. The president of the Brazilian Republic paused before signing his name to a document authorizing the use of a weapon, a weapon terrible in its effects but one that was the last defense of his nation. The seriousness of this national emergency had sent thousands of Brazilians to their churches to pray for God's help in their hour of need, and that help was now at hand.

The president didn't claim to speak for God Almighty, but he also believed that God helps those who help themselves. He looked at the faces around the long polished table. From the chief of staff of the armed forces to the archbishop, everyone looked grave. "Are you certain that we have no other hope?" he asked one last time.

The chief of staff shook his head. "We have been over the ground a hundred times and more, your excellency. We have no other way to protect ourselves. The TASA forces are too strong, and we have seen that we cannot put our fate in the hands of the Peacekeepers. If we are to continue to exist as a nation, we have no other choice."

The archbishop crossed himself before agreeing. "We have to protect the people, Don Pedro. We cannot allow this to happen without doing everything we can in our own defense."

In turn, the others echoed the chief of staff and archbishop's sentiments. After hearing from each man again, the president signed the document with a flourish and laid the pen down on the polished wood table. "It is done," he said, his voice grim. "May God help us."

God himself might not see fit to help them, but the Finger of God certainly would.

FIFTEEN HUNDRED MILES above the Earth, a dull black space vehicle hung in a geosynchronous orbit over the South American continent. Since the vehicle was well outside the orbit of the space stations and shuttle traffic, no one paid much attention to it. It was clear of the space traffic lanes and, to all intents and purposes, it was an abandoned derelict. It was a rather large derelict, that was true, but space was full of the derelicts and debris of seventy years of space exploration. As long as the space junk did not get in the way of the shuttle flights or the space-station orbits, it was usually ignored.

This particular piece of space junk was unmanned, but it was not abandoned; it was merely sleeping. A tight-beam, shielded comlink connected the vehicle with its controllers on the ground in Brazil. When orders from the Brazilian high command were flashed to the control center, the technicians in the remote location activated their controls to bring the space vehicle to life.

Power from fully charged solar accumulators surged through the lifeless craft. Relays and solenoids came to life, and solar panels unfolded like the wings of a bat to soak up the power of the sun. More power went to on-board computers and steering controls. In just a little under an hour, the vehicle's computers sent a signal to the ground that it was fully operational. When that signal arrived, the control center went into full operation and began putting the space craft to its intended use.

As per its instructions from the ground control station, the vehicle slowly swung its nose around until it was aimed at the gleaming white wheel of *La Reina*, the Argentinean space station hanging in orbit a thousand miles below. The orbiting scientific laboratory was the pride of Argentina and the source of much of her advanced technology. The products from its zero-gravity labs brought more than wealth to Argentina: it made her the leading power in South America.

Once the Brazilian space vehicle was locked on to its target, a compartment in the rear slowly opened. When the clamshell doors were fully retracted, a device raised itself on controllable arms and extended over the nose of the craft like a finger pointing from a fist. On command, relays tripped and solar-generated power surged through the device. The high-energy laser powered up and ran through a series of self-check programs.

When the ready signal was sent back to the ground control station, a weapons operator took command of the laser. Seated in a command chair in the hidden control facility, he slipped a cyberspace helmet down over his head and pulled a pair of cyberspace gloves onto his hands.

If the laser was named the "Finger of God," then he was the eye of God who would aim that finger.

The cyberspace helmet showed him the cold black of space as the backdrop to the bright points of light from the stars. It looked exactly as if he were in space with the laser. When he pointed the finger of his right hand, a glowing targeting ring was superimposed on his vision. Rolling his fist from side to side and rocking it back and forth moved the targeting ring.

His left hand controlled the targeting radar, and he quickly sought out his target. Blinking his right eye brought the gleaming white wheel of the Argentinean space station into his field of vision. Rolling his fist brought the targeting circle to bear on the space station.

After a final radar targeting pulse to achieve a positive lock on, the weapons operator made a trigger-pulling motion with his right index finger, and the laser fired.

The beam of ruby red coherent light flashed through space at the speed of light, 186,000 miles per second. Even though the beam had to travel almost a thousand miles to reach its target, to all practical purposes, it reached there instantaneously.

A six-inch circle on the gleaming white outer ring of the Argentinean space station suddenly glowed dull red. An instant later the internal atmospheric pressure blew through the weakened skin. The heated, moisture-laden air from inside the space station flash froze as it blasted into the cold vacuum of space.

Alarm bells echoed inside the station as the automatic pressure doors slammed shut to try to restore atmospheric integrity. The scientific crew looked up from their experiments and computer monitors in horror. The space station had been built to withstand the expected micrometeor strikes encountered by all space vehicles, but the fear of being hit by a meteor large enough to puncture the outer skin was always there.

The pressure alarm bells were still ringing inside the space station when the Brazilian weapons operator blinked his right eye again, bringing the orbiting lab even closer to him. Rolling his fist slightly, he aimed at his next target, the large observation dome in the central hub of the slowly revolving station. He squinted to align his targeting ring with the center of the dome, then his trigger finger twitched, and the laser fired again.

The eight-inch-thick clear plastic-and-sealant bubble of the dome resisted the laser longer than had the metal of the station's outer ring skin. The clear plastic passed most of the beam of light through it, dissipating it harmlessly.

The Brazilian weapons operator crooked his finger and held it back, causing the laser to fire repeatedly.

The solar power accumulators were fully charged so the weapon fired rapidly, cycling several times a minute.

Again most of the coherent light was passed through the clear plastic, but a certain amount of it was absorbed by the sealant between the layers of the plastic. As the sealant slowly heated and began to bubble, the laser light beam got a bite. And when it did, a six-inch circle of the observation dome glowed red for an instant before it burst.

Next to the mess hall, the observation deck was the most popular place on the station. The psychologists who had designed the station's living spaces had insisted that the crew would need it were they to maintain their mental health. Some of the off-duty crew came to gaze at the cold splendor of space while others came to look longingly downward at their ancestral home some five hundred miles below. The sudden decompression of the observation dome sucked several men and women into the cold, killing vacuum of space. They died before they could even scream.

After destroying the observation dome, the weapons operator switched his targeting ring and began systematically blasting the station to bits. When the laser beam focused on the external liquid-oxygen tanks, the resulting explosion shattered the symmetry of the slowly rotating ring in space. Another hit on the power accumulators continued the explosive disassembly of the station.

By the time the laser stopped firing, the space station had been blasted into so much orbiting space junk. A slowly expanding ring of twisted debris and the deep-space frozen bodies of the crew surrounded it like a halo.

The Finger of God had touched the pride of Argentina, and she was no more.

THE DESTRUCTION of the Argentinean space station ended Echo Company's brief respite from the war. Orders warning of imminent combat were flashed to the Peacekeeper units within an hour of the space laser's attack. Their holiday over, the grunts prepared to defend Brazil against an expected all-out TASA assault.

By this time, Spike Salazar had become a fixture around Echo Company. The congenial Brazilian officer had done everything in his power to make the time the Peacekeepers spent in his country enjoyable. As a result, Spike had become as close to the officers and grunts of Echo Company as any outsider ever could. Now, however, they looked at him in a very different light.

War was war—that they understood better than anyone on earth. Since Brazil had been attacked, she had the right to defend herself. But in their minds, war did not encompass the use of banned space weapons against a peaceful scientific space station. Wars were to be fought in the sand and mud of Earth or in her skies and seas. It was not to be fought in the cold vacuum of space.

The proper abode of the gods of war did not include the stars and planets.

THE DESTRUCTION of the Argentinean space station also ended the stalemate in the United Nations. The chambers of the UN roared with heated rhetoric about the Brazilian violation of the treaties regarding the peaceful use of space.

The Brazilian delegate, however, stood firm in his contention that his nation had the sovereign right to defend herself in any manner she saw fit. He further claimed that the space station had been armed with outlawed nuclear-warhead missiles, which was also in violation of the space treaties.

The Argentinean side angrily dismissed that claim as a blatant lie designed to excuse the Brazilian atrocity, quoting the UN inspection reports on the station. The Argentinean delegate demanded the immediate destruction of the Brazilian space weapons and swore vengeance for the twenty-four crewmen and women who had been killed.

The Brazilian delegate countered the Argentinean demand with a demand of his own. He said that the TASA forces were to immediately withdraw from Brazilian territory and leave their weapons and equipment behind. Failure to do so, he warned, would result in the laser being turned against selected ground targets, such as the Argentinean capital city of Buenos Aires.

The Argentinean delegate was silent for a moment, as if he was gathering his thoughts. He took a deep breath and calmly announced that if the Finger of God wasn't deactivated immediately, and the work done under close international supervision, his nation had no choice but to defend itself by any means at its disposal. Among those means they would employ, he said, were nuclear-armed ballistic missiles. He recommended the immediate evacuation of civilians from all Brazilian cities.

At that announcement, complete pandemonium broke out in the Security Council. The building's security guards were called in once more to restore order, but it proved not to be that easy. Fistfights had broken out on the floor of the Security Council, and it took quite some time to separate the combatants.

THAT NIGHT people all over the world looked up into the dark sky to try to see if they could spot the Brazilian Finger of God against the backdrop of stars. The space weapon was painted matt black, however, and did not reflect light. Like God, the laser was hidden from human sight.

16

Passo Fundo Valley—23 November

The expected TASA attack had not materialized, but the Peacekeepers had not stood down. The fact that they were ready to go into action instantly did not mean that the routine chores of any military unit had been put on hold. Quite the contrary. As far as Rosemont was concerned, it seemed that he had more bullshit paperwork to deal with than ever before.

The company commander was going over the weekly resupply request when his comlink beeped to indicate an incoming priority message. When he keyed his pad, the alphanumeric code "VS 374 H5X" appeared.

"Acknowledge Victor Sierra Three Seven Four Hotel Five Xray," he replied.

This was one battle-code message that Rosemont didn't need to look up to decipher. Every Peacekeeper knew the meaning of VS 374 H5X by heart. It was the code that warned they were under Situation Bright Red, the imminent use of outlawed battlefield nuclear weapons.

Rosemont took a quick moment to gather his thoughts. Drawing a deep breath, he keyed his mike implant and spoke. "All Bold elements, this is Bold Lancer. As of 0900 hours all USEF theater forces are under Situation Bright Red. Implement provisions of Situation Bright Red immediately. Acknowledge in turn."

"Bold Racer, affirm," Sullivan sent.

"Bold Cowboy, acknowledge," Stuart answered.

"Bold Strider, acknowledged," Ashley said, sounding shocked.

"Bold Thunder, affirm Bright Red," Rivera answered quickly.

"Bold Lancer Alpha, confirm Situation Bright Red." First Sergeant Ravenstein's voice was grim. "Implementing now."

Although nuclear weapons had been outlawed since 2004, the technology to make them was widely known. The traffic in nuclear materials was also closely controlled, but as with drug smuggling in the previous century, it had proven almost impossible to stop. If a nation was determined to get the material and information to build nukes, it could. The only proven deterrent was the certain knowledge that if it did, and it was found out, it would have Peacekeepers dropping in from out of the sky.

The example of Pakistan back in 2006 was kept fresh in everyone's minds as to what could happen if they dared to do the forbidden. The full fury of the Peacekeepers had been unleashed on Pakistan, and they had laid waste a large section of the country when they destroyed their nuclear arsenal. Until now no one in their right mind had wanted that treatment for their own nation.

The developed nations had been keeping a close eye on Argentina's growing and prosperous high-tech arms industry. Since it seemed to have been devoted to making first-class conventional weapons, no one had suspected them of flirting with nukes. It was a grave Intelligence failure and one that was going to cost lives.

The use of the Finger of God had been a serious escalation of the war, but this was even worse. No matter what had gone on before, it had been nothing compared to what could take place now. So far, the war had been fought in the United Nations as much as in Brazil. With the exception of the losses incurred in the territory occupied by the TASA forces, casualties had been few and for the most part had been confined to the combatants. There had been no mass destruction of civilian lives and property. That prospect had now changed. There was no way that nukes could be deployed without inflicting civilian casualties.

Worse than that, however, was the fear that if nuclear war did break out, it could not be contained. Many nations had bootleg nukes and, if they saw Argentina getting away with using them, they might take a chance on it, too. The nuclear peace that the Peacekeepers had fought so long to maintain was being threatened, and many feared that it would not last.

All over the world military forces went to Dep Two alert. If the specter of nuclear warfare was loose on the world again, they wanted to be prepared for it. Some nations dusted off their hidden nukes, while others put evacuation plans into effect.

In the Commonwealth of Independent States, the Russian Peacekeepers went to Dep One and prepared to move out to South America. The Peacekeepers, both Russian and American, had been formed to put an end to nuclear war. Now that it had been announced that Argentina was threatening to nuke Brazil, the Russians would not stand by idly and simply watch it happen. At least, not as long as the REF, the Russian Expeditionary Force, had anything to say about it.

If their American counterparts were laying it on the line again to protect the world from nuclear war, they would take their rightful place beside them.

THE MOOD in the force ops center was tense when Rosemont arrived for the briefing. The briefing room was crowded to overflowing, and everyone was talking in hushed tones as if they were at a funeral. Nodding to his fellow company commanders, Rosemont grabbed the last empty seat and sat down. "What's the word?" he whispered to the aviation company commander.

Hansen shrugged. "Fucked if I know."

"Ladies and gentlemen," the sergeant major announced. "The force commander."

Everyone rose to their feet when Colonel Jacobson walked to the front of the room. "Be seated, please," he said.

The colonel looked as if he had been up all night. His eyes were ringed with red, and his normally crisp uniform looked rumpled, as if he had slept in it. "I'll get right to the point. As all of you are well aware, the TASA high command has threatened to use nuclear weapons against Brazil unless the Finger of God space weapon is put out of commission immediately. We, of course, cannot allow that to happen."

A loud murmur of agreement came from the officers in the room.

"And," the colonel continued, "to keep it from happening, we are launching a two-pronged operation. Because we are already in Brazil, our task will be to find the ground control station for the Finger of God and put it out of action as soon as possible."

He paused. "While we are doing that, our Russian counterparts will be dealing with the Argentinean nuke weapons themselves."

A cheer broke out at the announcement that the Russians were coming.

"Even so, it will be a race against time and will require a maximum effort on everyone's part. Force Intel figures that the Argies can have their nukes operational in under forty-eight hours. And once they are ready for use, Intel feels that they will launch without further warning.

"Now, here comes the tricky part. We are not in a state of war with Brazil—" he paused and looked around "—yet. But because of the unusual circumstances, we have to act as if we are. Locate your Brazilian army liaison officers and place them under arrest. Do it politely, but arrest them and send them to our POW holding facility. They know too much about us, and we cannot allow them to pass any information to whoever is commanding the Finger of God.

"Regarding the Brazilian army during this operation, we will use rules-of-engagement Bravo. Do not initiate action against them as long as they stand aside and allow you to do your job. If it should become necessary to fire on them, try to inflict the minimum casualties possible while at the same time getting the situation under control."

He raised his hand to forestall the storm of protest that he knew would follow. The Peacekeepers operated on the pragmatic premise that when it became necessary to go to war, they went to war with no holds barred. Half measures and holding back were for the UN eunuchs or other politically driven forces. The USEF was the purest essence of war and had always operated that way. This, of course, was why they had been so successful, and to do anything less was to risk taking unnecessary casualties.

"I know what you are thinking," he said. "And I don't like it any more than you do. But this one time we will do it this way. Are there any questions at this point?"

His eyes swept the room. "If there are none, I will be followed by the ops officer."

Mad Mike also looked as if he had slept in his uniform, if in fact he had slept at all. "Okay, boys and girls," he said around the overly chewed cigar butt in his mouth, "here's the program. We have to find that laser's control center and take it out yesterday. Every minute it's in operation jeopardizes not only the population of Brazil, but ourselves, as well. Get out there and don't come back until you've put that damn thing out of action. If anyone or anything gets in the way of your conducting this operation, man, woman, child or beast, zero it and move on."

He allowed a slight smile to cross his face. "Keeping in mind, of course, that we originally came down here to protect the Brazilians from TASA aggression. As the colonel said, ROE Bravo is in effect, but don't let that slow you down. Find that control center and put it out of action before this whole Goddamn place goes up in a mushroom cloud."

MICK SULLIVAN MET Rosemont at the chopper pad when he returned and noticed that the company commander's face was grim. "What's the word, Major?"

"Where's Salazar?" Rosemont asked, ignoring his question.

"Probably over at the CP," Sullivan said.

"Grab two armed grunts and follow me."

"What's the problem?"

"We're at ROE Bravo with the Brazilians, and I have orders to place him under arrest and transport him to the force POW compound."

Sullivan whistled soundlessly. "Oh, shit!"

"My thoughts exactly."

Sullivan grabbed the first two grunts he saw and followed Rosemont over to the CP.

"Captain Salazar?"

Spike looked up, puzzled at Rosemont's formal tone. "Yes?"

"Because of the escalation of the conflict and the violation of the space nonproliferation treaty by your government, I have orders to place you under arrest and transport you to the USEF POW compound."

Spike was stunned. "I am sorry, Senhor Major," he said formally. "I do not know what to say."

"I'm sorry, too, Spike. I don't know what to tell you, but I have my orders."

Shooting a glance to the two grunts flanking Sullivan, Salazar realized that the Peacekeeper was serious. Moving slowly, he reached down and, unsnapping his pistol holster, carefully withdrew the weapon. Holding the pistol by the barrel, he stiffened to a position of attention as he handed it to Rosemont.

"Thank you, Captain Salazar," Rosemont said as he accepted the weapon. "I will return your side arm to you when the operation is over. I can assure you that you will be treated in accordance with the provisions of the London Accords. And if you like, I will inform your family where you are. "

"That won't be necessary, Major," the Brazilian said stiffly. "They will learn my fate soon enough when they hear that the Peacekeepers have turned against us."

When the grunts approached him with a set of plastic restraints, Rosemont waved them away. "The captain won't need those," he said.

Salazar's face was expressionless as he marched off between the two grunts.

"We're sure as hell not winning friends and influencing people here today, sir," Sullivan said, shaking his head as he followed Salazar with his eyes.

"You've got that shit right, Mick," Rosemont agreed. "But it's gone beyond that now. I'm afraid we're back to our usual configuration, us against everyone in sight."

"Ain't that the fucking truth."

ROSEMONT WAS HOLDING a mission briefing when his comlink beeped. "The Russian Third Company is dropping on Argentina right now, and the rest are following close behind them," he announced.

"The Third Company, that's Pavel Zerinski's bunch of maniacs, isn't it, sir?" Sullivan asked.

"Sure is," Rosemont replied. "I don't know if the Argies realize what they've gotten themselves in for."

Stuart laughed. "Lock up the women and children, the Cossacks are in town."

"That's for damn sure. I'd better put in an emergency supply request for an issue of vodka. I think we'll be needing it fairly soon."

Sullivan grinned. "Want to lay a little money on how long it will be before young Major Pavel Zerinski shows up around this place?"

Rosemont laughed and shook his head as he looked over at Ashley. "No thanks, Mick, that's a sucker's bet."

Ashley didn't blush, but she got a strange look on her face. Ashley and Echo Company had met the smooth-talking Russian Peacekeeper officer when his unit had come to their rescue in Laos the month before. When it was all over, he had been so taken with her that he had almost gone AWOL rather then leave her presence.

"'Was this the face that launched a thousand ships and burnt the topless towers of Ilium?'" Mick quoted as he bowed in Ashley's direction.

"That's Homer, isn't it?" Rosemont asked.

Mick shook his head. "Nope. The reference is to Helen of Troy, of course, but it's by the English poet Christopher Marlowe and it's about his girlfriend."

"I'm impressed, Mick." Rosemont laughed. "I thought all you studied was old war movies."

He shrugged. "The legacy of a youth misspent in private schools, I'm afraid, sir. My father wanted me to be a professor of English literature, and I've never gotten over it. In fact, it was studying English poetry that drove me to seek refuge in old war movies."

"You keep quoting poetry around here, and the Old Man will pull you back to headquarters with the rest of his collection of intellectuals for a staff rat job."

Sullivan didn't have to fake a shudder. "Bite your tongue, Major, that's a fate worse than death."

Rosemont laughed; staff work never did appeal to die-hard grunts. "Don't worry, Mick, I won't let him take you. I need you to keep us stocked with vodka for the Russians."

"If you two are done, sir," Ashley snapped, "maybe we can get on with this fucking briefing? My people and I have got work to do today."

"Sorry, Ash," Rosemont said as he went back to assigning the search sectors.

When the briefing was over, Ashley left without a word to get her recon teams ready to go to the field. The tilt of her head and the set of her jaw showed that she was pissed to the max.

"She's a little touchy about Zerinski, isn't she?" Sullivan commented as he watched her march away.

Rosemont had to agree, but now that he had been sharing Ashley's bed for the past month, he had a better understanding of why she didn't appreciate the male attention that her looks inevitably brought her. Unlike most women, she felt that her beauty was a hindrance to getting her job done, rather than a help.

"She'll get over it soon enough," he said. "But if Zerinski shows up before she does, he'll be in for a royal ass-kicking if he's not careful."

"I'd give my next paycheck to see that one," Mick chuckled.

"That makes two of us."

17

Northern Argentina—23 November

The Russian Peacekeepers' capsule drop on northern Argentina was not the piece of cake that the early-morning surprise American drop on southern Brazil had been. They had to take their drop zones the old-fashioned way—they fought for them.

Following their long flight across the Atlantic, the Russian Expeditionary Force's swing-wing, super-sonic troop transports had landed at an American Air Force base in Florida. After a quick refueling and servicing, they continued flying down the east coast of South America. As they approached the coast of Argentina, they picked up an escort of two dozen American Navy F/A-38 Puma carrier-based fighters from the USS *Reagan* to run interference for them. The fighter cover was going to be needed.

The Argentineans knew that the Russian Peace-keepers were coming. They also knew what they were coming for and they were not about to roll over and play dead for them. They needed to buy time so they could get their hidden nuke missiles operational and they threw their small air force into the air to try to stop the Russians.

Though the TASA land forces were top rate by anyone's standards, other than the Peacekeepers', Argentina did not have a world-class air force. None of their neighbors, and potential enemies, had strong air arms, so the TASA command had not seen the need to spend the money on sophisticated fighter interceptors for their air force. Instead, they had concentrated on Tac Air ground-attack aircraft to support their armored forces and had left the air-defense mission to ground-based anti-aircraft missiles. These missile batteries went on full alert when the transports were still well out to sea. Powering up their targeting radars, they swept the skies looking for the invaders.

Led by the Navy's electronic countermeasures planes and a Puma Wild Weasel flight, the combined Russian-American strike force approached the Argentinean coastline at a speed of Mach 1.5. They were just crossing the coast when the airborne warning and control, or AWAC, aircraft orbiting over the South Atlantic flashed a warning that Argentinean jet fighters were vectoring in on an interception course. The fighter Pumas immediately broke away from the formation, broke Mach 2.5 and went to work.

The Pumas quickly swept the sky of the handful of jet fighters the Argentineans sent up. It wasn't a fair fight. The Pumas with their sophisticated weapons-control systems, their stealthing systems and their supersonic vectoring engines could not be bested by last year's jet fighters. In a matter of a few short minutes, the only aircraft left in the skies over Argentina wore the markings of the Peacekeepers.

With the missiles' targeting radars being jammed by the Navy's ECM birds, the Puma Wild Weasel flight went to work eliminating the TASA air-defense batteries. This was a little more tricky, and the attacking force took hits before they were able to knock out all of the missile sites. As before, though the TASA missiles were good, they simply were not good enough to deal with the latest Anti-Radiation Cruise Missiles, ARCMs, carried by the Wild Weasels.

After they were fired, these missiles loitered in the sky at subsonic speeds until a missile battery used its radar to lock on to one of the attacking planes. Then the ARCM locked the radar's position in its nav computers, went to Mach 2 and dived into the radar site. Even if the radar was turned off, it didn't matter; the location was fixed in its computer nav system and they never missed.

While the fighters and attack planes cleared the way, the transports went on to their preplanned drop zones. The Russian Expeditionary Force was almost twice the size of the American Peacekeepers and included two armor companies of heavily armed, air-droppable skimmers, as well as their hulk heavy infantry. Because of their size, they hit three drop zones at the same time.

The first capsules out of the planes were the Russian light infantry grunts. Riding their capsules all the way down until the last possible second as if they were bombing the DZs, the Russians hit hot DZs. Each drop zone was on or near a TASA military site so the landings were not unopposed. In fact, the Argies fought hard to deny the footholds to the Russians, but with support from the attack Pumas, the Russians were able to carve out small perimeters and hold them for the second drop.

The Russian heavy infantry dropped out of the sky on the next run over the DZs. Once the powered fighting suits were on the ground and in action, the situation turned around abruptly. Cannons and rocket launchers blazing, the Boris the Bear suits quickly drove the counterattacking Argies back beyond small-arms range so the transports could make their last drops.

The final low-level drop delivered the skimmers of the Russians' armor companies and the support troops. Now the Russians were ready to continue the operation. Quickly mounting their skimmers, they drove on to their objectives.

Their bellies empty, the Russian transports turned back to the Atlantic for their rendezvous with the aerial tankers sent up by the American Navy. Once they were refueled, they would head north, back to the air base in Florida to await the outcome of the operation.

WHILE THE RUSSIANS established their bloody footholds in northern Argentina, the USEF continued the systematic search for the laser control station in Brazil. For Rosemont and Echo Company, it had been a frustrating exercise. By the end of the first twenty-four hours of beating the bushes, they had very little to show for their efforts.

Every one of Rosemont's recon teams was out in the jungle or in the air searching for any sign of the Finger of God's ground-control facility. He had even broken his infantry platoons down into search teams to supplement the recon grunts. But so far, all anyone had found was empty hostile jungle and inhospitable natives.

The other Peacekeeper units working the Brazilian towns and cities had seen a little more action, but with no better results. Now that the Brazilian forces had turned semihostile, the Peacekeepers had lost their local guides and were working on their own. They had also gotten into a few scattered firefights with Brazilian outposts and garrisons who did not seem to understand that the Peacekeepers were determined to conduct their searches no matter what.

Following the colonel's strict guidelines about inflicting the minimum number of casualties on the Brazilian forces, they had taken more casualties themselves than they were accustomed to taking. But the Brazilian military hadn't turned completely hostile yet, and as long as they weren't trading rounds with them full-time, the situation wasn't completely untenable. It was just a royal pain in the ass, and time was running out. Force Intel had estimated that they had only forty-eight hours to find and eliminate the laser before the Argies got their missiles operational.

All this meant to Rosemont was that he was sitting back at his CP coordinating the search efforts and acting as information central for the search teams. Most of Rivera's weapons platoon gunners had stayed behind to provide security for the company CP and man the comlinks.

First Sergeant Ravenstein was giving Rosemont a welcome hand with these chores. Having worked in operations before he came to Echo Company, he was very good at this short of thing, better than Rosemont, actually. Hawk Ravenstein was working out well as the company's new first sergeant, but Rosemont still missed having his old top sergeant, Big Daddy Ward, around the CP.

Ward had been killed the previous month in the Cambodian jungle, and his death was still being mourned in Echo Company. Ward had been a fixture around the company for many years, and much of what was best about the unit had come about because of his patient, competent leadership.

But losses were a fact of life in the military, and Ravenstein had stepped in and was now putting his own distinctive mark on the company. Ward would not be soon forgotten, but Ravenstein was welcome.

TWISTING THE THROTTLE of his OH-39 Bubble Top hard up against the stop, USEF First Lieutenant Gunner Thompson nudged the cyclic control stick forward while simultaneously slamming it all the way over to the right. The small recon scout ship went up on one side as it dodged around a towering tree at well over two hundred and fifty miles per hour. Once past the obstacle, the chopper's belly was back down on the treetops again.

In the left-hand seat, Kat Wallenska surged against her shoulder harness when the ship leveled out again. While the ground teams searched the more likely places for the laser control station, Kat and Thompson were making a preliminary aerial recon of the jungle in northwestern Brazil before moving her team in on foot.

"Why don't you drop this fucking thing down a little lower, Gunner?" she growled. "So I can just get out and do the recon on foot."

Thompson laughed. "You know the drill, Kat. On the deck and put your boot in it."

"I'm going to put my boot up your ass if you crash us, is what I'm gonna do."

Gunner grinned broadly behind his helmet visor. High-speed, low-altitude recon was his favorite pastime. The OH-39 NOTAR—no tail rotor—Bubble Top scout chopper was not only fast, but it was also the most maneuverable helicopter that had ever been built. The combination of the rigid main rotor and jet-thrust directional-control design allowed the ship to do things that had once been the sole privilege of small fixed-wing aerobatic aircraft.

Along with the scout ship's high speed and high maneuverability went a full package of both recon sensors and ground-attack weapons. If Gunner came across a target, he wouldn't have to run for cover and call the big boys in to take it out, but could deal with it himself.

The jungle below Kat was much the same as what they had spent the past two hours looking at, an endless tract of almost featureless green canopy. As far as she was concerned, it was a complete waste of time to bother with it. But the orders from Mad Mike had been explicit: every single square meter of this country was to be searched until they found what they were looking for.

Gunner completed his run and pulled the Bubble Top up in a swooping climb. "Okay, Kat," he said. "What's next? I've got enough fuel to cover one more sector before we have to go back."

Kat consulted her nav screen. The next two sectors were the same as this one, featureless flat jungle canopy. The third one, however, had a few volcanic peaks in the middle and the jungle looked a bit thinner. The map also showed an old road running through the middle of it.

"Let's try sector Kilo Five One next," she said. "If it looks good, I can call in the rest of the team and we can stretch our legs while you go back and top off."

"Sounds good to me, Kat," Thompson said as he kicked the tail around to head north. "I need a pit stop and a cup of coffee myself."

ROSEMONT DRAINED the last of the coffee from the Readi Heat canister and tossed it onto the growing pile of empties. He hated sitting around waiting for something to happen and he wasn't too sure how much more caffeine he could stomach. He was just popping the top on another coffee canister when the first sergeant hurried up to him with a hard copy in his hand.

"We've got a report on another possible site, sir," Ravenstein said.

"What is it this time, Hawk," Rosemont growled, "another goddamn weather-reporting station?"

The worst thing about this operation was that every time the search teams turned up a remote building with a satcomlink antenna sticking out of the roof, everyone jumped through their ass to check it out. Most of the sites, however, turned out to be merely holovee satellite antennae. A few had been weather satellite-reporting-stations, while others had been commercial links.

Force headquarters was getting tired of sending their overworked tech teams out only to find that the suspect was innocent. Mad Mike had been ragging on everyone's ass this morning about that topic, as well as several others. Rosemont wasn't the only Peacekeeper who was tired of waiting. Everyone wanted this wrapped up before it got even more serious.

"This one just might be different, sir," the first sergeant replied. "It's a camouflaged-tight beam dish with a retransmission unit sitting all by itself on a mountaintop, and it's aimed out at the jungle."

That sounded a little more promising. "Who found it?"

"Strider Alpha."

Leave it to Kat Wallenska to turn up something worth looking into. Rosemont parked his coffee, stood up and reached for his assault harness.

"If there's nothing coming up that needs my immediate attention, Top," he said, "maybe I should go take a look at this one myself."

The first sergeant knew that Rosemont was going crazy sitting around the CP and just wanted an excuse to get away for a while. "Go ahead, sir. There's nothing going here on that I can't take care of myself."

Rosemont had snatched up his weapon and was running for the chopper pad before Top Ravenstein had even finished speaking. Boarding the waiting Bubble Top, he quickly flashed Kat's find to the pilot's nav display.

"Got it," the pilot said, watching the coordinates come up.

"Let's get it, then."

The pilot immediately pulled pitch on his collective control, and the small chopper leaped up into the sky. Pushing down on the rudder pedals, he snapped the tail around and twisted his throttle hard up against the stop. In a few seconds the screaming turbines had accelerated the ship to its top speed.

Rosemont settled in for the one-hour flight. He didn't want to get his hopes up too high, but Kat had been known to produce miracles before. He only hoped that she was on target again. Even if she wasn't, it sure as hell beat sitting around the CP for another day while everyone else was out enjoying themselves in the field.

18

In the Jungle—24 November

As the Bubble Top pilot flew low over the jungle, Rosemont scanned the terrain below. It didn't look promising. All he saw was an unbroken carpet of green jungle canopy. But he also knew that if he had to hide a secret military facility he couldn't think of a better place than in the middle of an uninhabited tropical rain forest.

The question was, though, if the control center was out here, how was it kept supplied and serviced? That would be the key to finding it. If he could locate the road, landing pad or river that allowed men and material to be brought out he would find it.

"We're coming up on the hill, sir," the pilot said. "And I've got someone spotted on the ground waiting for us."

"Put it down anywhere you can."

The scout ship flared out for a landing on a bare patch on the side of the hill. Balancing the ship on one skid, the pilot held his machine in a hover while Rosemont stepped out. As soon as he was clear, the Bubble Top lifted off and dropped back down on the deck for the return flight. Blade time was at a premium right now, and he couldn't wait around while Rosemont went about his business. When the company commander was finished, he'd come back, but he had another mission to fly in the meantime.

Kat Wallenska was wearing a big grin as she stepped up to meet him. "I think we've found it, Major."

"I sure as hell hope so, Kat," Rosemont said. "Lead me to it."

Kat's find was right beyond a thick screen of brush at the eastern crest of the small hill. Though Rosemont wasn't a comotech, it sure as hell looked as if it was a tight-beam retransmission station to him. The camouflaged twin-antennae dishes were a dead giveaway. One of the antennae pointed up into space, while the other one looked out over the jungle canopy to the north.

While the retrans site was well camouflaged from aerial observation, it had an unobscured shot to a small hill in the valley below some three thousand meters away. The hill the one antenna was aimed at was not a particularly impressive terrain feature, a bald, low mound probably of volcanic origin. It did not need to be big; all it needed to have was a clear shot to the retrans dish, and that it had.

"How'd you happen to find this thing anyway?" he asked Kat.

The recon sergeant grinned. "Pure blind luck, Major, no skill or techie gadgets involved this time. It was raining earlier, you know, a fine misty rain, and the sun was out at the same time making a rainbow. I looked at the end of the rainbow through the imagers and saw the antenna dish.''

It was nice to see that even on a high tech-battlefield luck still had a place of honor. ''The pot of gold at the end of the rainbow.''

''I sure as hell hope so, sir,'' Kat replied. ''You going to call it in?''

Rosemont shook his head. ''Not till we check it out first. Mad Mike's really got a case of the red ass today. He's tired of us sending his tech teams out on wild-goose chases. I'm not going to bother him with this unless it proves promising. That means that you and I are going down there and take a look at that hill ourselves.''

''That's fine with me, Major.''

Rosemont called up a map on his visor tacscreen and saw that there was an access route close to the target area, a logging road three klicks to the east of the hill. According to the map, the road was marked as being abandoned, but since the map had originated from Brazilian sources, that could very well be purposeful misinformation. If the hill did contain the hidden laser control center he was looking for, he could hardly expect the Brazilians to advertise its presence on a map.

The map also didn't show a side road or even a trail leading from the logging road to the hill, but that didn't mean that a path hadn't been cut under the jungle canopy. The canopy was so thick it could hide any number of supply roads or trails. The fact that the main logging road terminated a couple klicks farther

on and there were no signs of logging activities anywhere in the vicinity only lent credibility to his theory.

It could be just another false alarm, but it was the
best shot anyone in Echo Company had come up with
in the past twenty-four hours. And with time running
out, it was certainly worth investigating.

Rosemont looked around at the four grunts of Kat's
Strider Alpha team and decided he wanted to have a
little more backup in case this did turn out to be the
pot of gold. "Who's closest to us right now?" he
asked.

Kat consulted her tacscreen. "Bold Strider and the
Strider Charlie team are in sector Whiskey Two Seven
and Strider Bravo is working Yankee Three Niner."

Since it might be a good idea to have another officer on hand in case it really was the control center and
everything turned to shit when they went in, he decided to invite Ashley and the Strider Charlie team in
to assist him with this little operation. The fact that he
hadn't seen her in the past few days hadn't even
crossed his mind as he'd gone through his decision-
making process.

"Bold Strider," he keyed his mike implant and
transmitted. "Bold Lancer."

"Strider, go," Ashley answered instantly.

"Lancer. I need you and Strider Charlie at Alpha's
location. She's found something that looks promising, and I want some backup."

"Strider affirm. I have the Bubble Tops coming in
now and I'll divert to your area."

"Lancer, affirm. We'll be waiting."

While he waited for Ashley and her team to arrive, Rosemont made a full sensor scan of the hill, but his readouts showed him nothing out of the ordinary. Again, though, he was not surprised. If the Brazilians were advanced enough to have built and launched a space laser weapon in secret, they would certainly be capable enough to mask its control center from detection.

The more he found nothing, however, the more he felt that this was in fact the place they were looking for.

WHEN ASHLEY SCRAMBLED out of her Bubble Top, Rosemont could tell that she was ready to go to war. He had seen that tight smile on her face and the glitter in her eyes many times before and knew what it meant. Like the rest of them, she was also tired of waiting and was anxious to go to work, wrap up things and go home.

"What do you have, Alex?" As always, Ashley got straight to the point when it involved business.

"I'm not sure, Ash," he answered. "But that's what we're going to go down there to find out."

He quickly briefed her on Kat's discovery of the tight-beam retrans antennae and the hill it was aimed at. She looked thoughtful for a moment. "It sounds good to me," she said. "There's got to be a damn good reason that they're sending tight-beam transmissions to a hill way the hell out here in the middle of nowhere."

"That's exactly what I was thinking. Even if it isn't the laser control station, I'm betting that it's something we'll be interested in."

"Let's go take a look at it, then."

Rosemont quickly briefed the grunts of the two recon teams. The object of the exercise was simple: get down there and carefully search the hill and its surrounding area for anything out of the ordinary. If they found anything, they'd pull back quickly and call for help. It was a routine sneak-and-peek recon mission, and they'd all done it hundreds of times before.

"If these guys do have their ground-control station set up down there," Rosemont said, "I expect that they'll have the entire area saturated with sensors and detectors. So we're going to have to be as careful as we can on the way in. No comlinks and no sensors, hand and arm signals only. In fact, I want you to switch everything off so we don't show even any residual EM radiation."

The Peacekeepers' comlinks and battlefield electronics were well shielded to prevent hostile detection. But there was always the chance that something wasn't working properly or that the enemy had extra-sensitive detectors that could pick up EM signal leak.

"However," he continued, "when the shit hits the fan, everything goes back on immediately. We get the hell outta there and scream for help."

He looked around at the recon grunts. "Does anyone have any questions?"

As he had expected, there were no questions. The briefing had been short because there was no way that

he could foresee everything that might happen once
they moved out and closed in on the hill. Even so, he
was confident that whatever did happen down there,
they would be able to deal with it. They were the
Peacekeepers, the ultimate professionals on the battlefield.

"Okay, people," Rosemont said. "Let's get down
there and do it."

AFTER A FINAL CHECK of their weapons and equipment, the ten Peacekeepers moved out. It took them
about twenty minutes to make their way down the side
of the hill with the retrans unit on top. Once they got
down onto the flat between the two hills, the first
thousand meters was as easy as a walk in a jungle
park. With their chameleon suits dialed to muted jungle tones, they slipped through the lush undergrowth
like quick-moving mottled green shadows.

In a movement to contact like this, they were in a
line formation with Kat up on the point. Rosemont
was walking her slack, and Ironstone was backing him
up. Ash and the Strider Charlie team pulled drag, a
hundred meters behind the Strider Alpha team.

Without her sensors to give her early warning of
trouble, Kat was extremely careful as she made her
way through the brush. Like Rosemont, she felt that
this was the place, and if it was, it was certain to be
well protected. After they advanced more than a klick
toward their objective, however, she was beginning to
wonder if this was going to pan out. So far, she had

seen nothing to indicate that humans had ever been this way before.

Coming to a faint path crossing her front, she automatically dropped into cover to check it out. Although it ran straight for quite a few meters, it looked like just another animal trail to her. She stood up and was just about to step out to cross the trail when she saw a faint scuff mark in the trail in front of her. The mark had a hard ridge on one side that was not made by an animal's paw. It could have been made by a combat boot, though.

Kat froze and looked up and down the trail. Even though it appeared to be clear, she stayed frosty and continued looking for something else out of place, something that hadn't grown there with the rest of the jungle. Halfway up a tree to her right front, she saw it. A small matte box mottled with brown, gray and green was nestled in the crotch of a tree.

The three thin wire antennae sticking out of the top of the box identified it as an electronic sensor. Had she been using her battlefield electronics, this thing probably would have picked it up. Once more Rosemont had accurately called the shot.

Kat cautiously backed away from the tree until she was safely under cover. Slowly turning around, she waved Rosemont forward to have a look himself. The company commander slid in beside her a moment later. "What'd you have?" he whispered in her ear.

"Electronic sensor," she whispered back, and pointed.

Rosemont confirmed her identification and pulled back. Using hand and arm signals, he sent Ash and her team around to his left flank to find a way past the sensor. When she signaled that she had found a way around it, he pulled Kat's team out and followed in Ash's trail. As soon as they had caught up with her, he had Kat take up the point again.

He signaled Ash to close in tight on Strider Alpha's drag so the two teams wouldn't get separated if they got jumped. Now that they had found the outer ring of the hostile defenses, they would have to be even more cautious. This was looking better and better every minute, and he didn't want to screw it up now.

The next thousand meters went much more slowly than the first as Kat carefully picked her way through the undergrowth, but she saw no further signs of human activity. When they had closed to within six hundred meters of the base of the hill, Rosemont called a halt. He wanted to take a real close look at the area before they moved in any closer.

Ten pairs of eyes thoroughly searched the area between them and the base of the hill. When they saw nothing out of the ordinary, Rosemont signaled them to move on in. They had just broken cover when a shot rang out. Donelson, the grunt to Kat's left, cried out as the round took him high in the chest.

"Cover!"

A flurry of fire from their left front followed the first shot. All the grunts had reached cover and automatically went into their counterambush drill.

The Brazilians obviously had more than just electronic defenses guarding this remote hill. They had the bare eyeballs of riflemen out here, as well. This was the hidden laser control facility. All they had to do now was get the hell out of here and call in the dogs.

At the first shot, Ironstone immediately went into action with his sniper's rifle. Powering up the ranging scope, he scanned the terrain where the fire was coming from. A flash of movement caught his eyes, and he focused in on it. The scope showed him the upper torso of a man in a mottled jungle camouflage uniform. He triggered the rifle, and the figure went down.

A barrage of return fire forced him back down quick. The rest of the grunts were returning full-auto counterambush fire but were having little result. They were badly outnumbered. Their comlinks and sensors back on, Rosemont ordered a retreat.

Just then a second bunch of Brazilians opened up from the way they had come, blocking their escape route. Rosemont was organizing a defense in place when Kat called over the comlink. "Major," she said, "look at that rock outcropping at the base of the hill. It looks like there's a door in the middle of it."

Rosemont looked with his helmet imagers and saw that Kat was right. It did look as though there was a camouflaged door. "Follow me!" he shouted as he raced for the hidden opening.

Dragging the wounded Donelson with them, the recon grunts followed after him.

19

Under the Hill—24 November

After the bright sun outside, it took a few seconds for the Peacekeepers' eyes to adjust to the darkness inside the door. "Everyone get in okay?" Rosemont asked.

"Donelson's hit," Kat answered. "But we're all inside."

A burst of fire hit the outside of the door, and a bullet ricocheted off the rock wall of the corridor. One of the recon grunts stuck the barrel of his LAR around the corner of the door and ripped off a long burst. Another one dropped to Donelson's side to treat his wound.

When his eyes adjusted to the dim light, Rosemont saw that they were in a corridor cut into the bare rock. A dozen meters farther on, it looked as if there was another door.

"Ironstone," Rosemont ordered. "Keep 'em busy outside. Kat, Ashley, bring two men and let's try that other door."

Rosemont couldn't see any security monitors covering the door and decided to charge it before anyone inside realized that company was coming. With Kat and Ashley flanking him on either side, he undogged the door and flung it open.

A man in a white lab coat over a khaki uniform raised a submachine gun when the door crashed open, but Kat cut him down with a short burst of 5 mm fire before he could shoot. By the time the sound of the shots faded, the other half-dozen men in the room all had their hands raised high over their heads.

"Get these guys outta here," Rosemont shouted to the grunts.

Prodding them with the muzzles of their rifles, the two grunts herded the technicians out of the main room and into the corridor leading to the outside.

Looking around, Rosemont was surprised at what he saw. Rather than the complicated control center he had expected with neat rows of control desks, monitors and sophisticated equipment, this was a spartan facility. Naked power cables stretched across the crudely leveled rock floor. Computer monitors, filing cabinets and desks were scattered all around the room. These guys weren't going to win any good-house-keeping awards for this setup, but the place looked serviceable.

In the center of the room was a large control chair. On the seat of the chair was a cyberspace helmet and a pair of cyberspace control gloves. For a moment he was puzzled at seeing them there, then it hit him. They were using a cyberspace computer to control the Finger of God.

When he thought about it, it made sense. With the operator and the weapon both tied together in a cyberspace construct, he would be able to aim and fire the laser space weapon as easily as if it were a rifle or a pistol.

"Alex, quick!" Ashley called out urgently from one of the monitor stations on the other side of the room, "We've got company coming!"

Rosemont hurried over to where she was sitting behind a monitor and keyboard. "How did you get that thing working? I didn't know that you could read Portuguese."

"I don't have to," she said, sounding disgusted. "This whole setup is in English. All the fucking equipment and programs were made in the good 'ole U.S. of A. We've been selling this shit to the wrong people again."

The monitor showed at least a full company of jungle infantry quickly moving in to surround the base of the hill. They were heavily armed and moving fast.

Rosemont's eyes flicked back to the cyberspace control station in the middle of the room. If all the computers and software were American, there was no reason he couldn't use them himself. He was trained in cyberspace equipment and was one of the handpicked officers and NCOs who had undergone deep-space combat training in the cyber tank. Compared to fighting in a space suit, the laser controls couldn't be that complicated.

"I think that I can control that laser," he said.

"What!"

"Yes." He pointed over to the control chair. "I think that cyberspace setup over there runs the Finger of God. And—" he smiled thinly "—if it does, I can control it as well as they did."

"But what are you going to do with it?"

"I'm going to see if I can't get that laser to blast those guys moving in on us." He paused. "And when I'm done with that, I'm going to see if I can't use it to put this place out of action once and for all. That laser will probably cut into this hill like it was soft cheese."

"You're not serious!"

"Yes, I am, Ash," he said, his face set. "Look, we can't get reinforcements here in time to keep them from taking this place back from us. And if they do, they might turn the laser on us. I've got to put this thing out of action now, and it's the only thing I can do it with."

"We can try to damage the control room."

"I thought of that, but then we'd be stuck in here with no way out. Also, they probably have backup systems for the laser, and we might not get to all of them. But if I'm in the chair controlling the damn thing, I'll sure as hell be able to handle this situation." He smiled. "That's why they call it the Finger of God."

"I'm not going to leave you here." Ashley's voice was low and final.

Rosemont kept his own voice level in return. This was not the best time in the world to be having a lovers' spat. "I'm giving you an order, Captain. Get the people out of here. Now! I don't know the blast effect of this thing, so clear 'em out to at least five hundred meters.''

Ashley's eyes flashed. "Fuck your orders, Alex. I'm not leaving you here, and that's that."

Rosemont looked over at Kat. She was keeping her face neutral and trying to stay out of it. "Sergeant Wallenska," he said. "I'm ordering you to escort Captain Wells out of this complex immediately. Shoot her in the legs and drag her out if you have to, but get her ass out of here. Now!"

Kat didn't flinch under the lash of Rosemont's voice. "That's most affirm, sir."

The recon sergeant turned to her platoon leader. "Come on, Ash. You heard the man, move it."

When Ashley didn't respond, Kat raised her LAR. "You know I'll shoot if I have to, Ash, so let's get it in gear."

Ash's face fell and she turned back to Rosemont.

"Go, love," he said. "Please."

AFTER CLOSING the control-room door behind them, Rosemont dogged the locks tight before returning to the cyberspace control console. He checked to see that the cyberspace computer program was still running, then slid into the command chair. He slipped the cyberspace helmet onto his head, dropped the helmet visor over his face and slid his hands into the control gloves.

Calling up the cyberspace menu on his visor, he saw that it was pretty much the same as the one he had

trained with back at Fort Benning. He activated the
program and found himself in a new kind of cyberspace. He was well experienced with the cyberspace
tanks at Benning, but this was a completely different
situation. In the tanks he was simply a man who had
been placed into a different environment. Here it was
as if he had become a god. He was hanging in the air
a thousand feet above the control complex, and the
cyberspace computer gave him a godlike view of the
area around the hill. No wonder the Brazilians had
named this the Finger of God.

Dragging Donelson with them, the grunts trying to
fight their way out and the attacking Brazilians were
as clear to his eyes as if he were hovering over them in
a helicopter. But it was better than being in a Bubble
Top because he had a panoramic view completely
unobstructed by a surrounding aircraft. His vision was
so clear that he could even distinctly see Ashley, Kat
and the grunts. Ash had retrieved her LAR and she
was fighting alongside the recon sergeant.

When he saw a platoon of Brazilian infantry working their way around on their flank, he instinctively
shouted a warning to Ash. The sound of his muffled
voice inside the helmet brought him back to the reality of the situation. He thought of trying to get
through to her on his comlink, but if he took off the
cyberspace helmet, he would lose his ability to see
what was happening. Also he wasn't sure that he could
get a comlink signal through the control center's EMR
shielding. But since he was now controlling the Finger of God, he could use it to help her.

He frantically scanned the menu displayed along the bottom of his visor looking for instructions on how to fire the laser, but there were none. He stopped and thought for a moment about why the Brazilians called the weapon the Finger of God. That had to be significant. If the laser was God's finger, all he should have to do was point his finger and fire.

He pointed his right index finger like a pistol. Suddenly a glowing red sight ring was superimposed on the ground below him. He centered the pip in the ring on his target and squeezed his right trigger finger, hoping that there wasn't some kind of interlock that prevented the laser from firing so close to its own control facility.

There wasn't, and the laser fired.

The first shot hit at the front of the hostile formation. The effect of the laser beam was like an artillery shell landing in the middle of them. There was no shrapnel, of course, but the intense heat made trees explode and rocks burst as the water inside them was instantly turned into superheated steam.

The Brazilians dived for cover, but there was no escaping the Finger of God. Rosemont shifted his point of aim and fired again. The beam caught one of the Brazilians directly, and he burst into flames. His comrades recoiled in horror and looked to the heavens. The laser touched down again, and they broke and ran. Dropping their weapons, they scattered into the brush as fast as they could run.

WHEN ROSEMONT SAW that Ashley and the grunts were well out of danger and clear of the hill, it was time to see if he could destroy the control center he sat in. First, though, he wanted to see what this Finger of God was capable of. This was the most fantastic sensation he had ever experienced, and he was reluctant to leave it.

He zoomed higher up into the atmosphere and found himself on the edge of space. Looking up, he saw the bright points of light that were the stars against the velvet blue-black of space. The flash of a satellite moving through space caught his eye and he brought it into focus. Pointing his finger displayed the firing circle. All he would have to do was crook his finger and the satellite would die.

Looking back down to Earth, he saw the deep green of the rain forest jungle below and the muddy ribbon of the Amazon River. Zooming down like a falling star, he stopped a thousand feet above the hill. Ashley and the grunts were well clear of it now, so it was time to go to work. He centered the cross hairs on the peak of the hill and fired.

Through the helmet, he saw the laser beam touch down. And everywhere it touched, destruction followed. Trees and brush instantly burst into flame. Suddenly heated rocks exploded, causing landslides. Deep in the control room, he could not hear, but he felt the rumble as the laser beam bit deeper into the top of the hill. In cyberspace, he saw the volcanic rock glow dull red as if it was back inside the volcano that had given it birth. In places, the rocks were heated to the point that they actually flowed like lava.

Rosemont kept his trigger finger crooked to the full-automatic-fire position. Powered by the solar accumulators on the space craft, the laser cycled at its fastest rate, firing once every ten seconds. The effect was like an endless barrage of EHE artillery rounds. Each time the beam touched down, more rocks burst from internal steam before glowing red.

By now the laser had carved a small crater into the top of the hill, but he kept his trigger finger down. He would continue firing the laser until he either flattened the hill or the weapon stopped firing.

Suddenly, he felt a crash in the control room and he was sitting back in the control chair, his eyes blind inside the blank helmet and his hands encased in dead cyber control gloves. Ripping the cyberspace helmet off, he coughed. The dark room was filled with hot, choking smoke and dust. If he was going to get out of here alive, he'd better get his ass in gear ASAP.

Dropping to the floor, he felt around for his LAR and combat helmet. He found the rifle, but couldn't locate his helmet. Struggling to breathe, he stopped fumbling around for it and started for the door. In the dark he ran into several decks and computer stations before reaching the wall. Trying to remember where the door was, he started feeling his way along the wall, searching.

He had chosen the right direction and located the door within a few meters. The door frame had been sprung in the destruction and he had to fight the dogs

to unlock it and swing it far enough open to squeeze
through. The air in the corridor leading outside wasn't
any better than the air in the control room had been.

He was starting to feel the effects of the smoke and
dropped to his hands and knees. The air was no
clearer, but it was cooler to his lungs, and he started
crawling. Kat had left the outer door partially open,
and he could see a faint bar of light through the smoke
and dust. All he had to do was keep crawling toward
the light and he would make it.

The corridor was littered with rocks broken loose
from the roof, and he kept running into them. When
he crawled around them, the light from the door kept
him oriented in the right direction, but it didn't look
as if he was getting any closer to it. His lungs were
burning and he was having trouble seeing, but he kept
on crawling.

He opened his eyes when he bumped against something in front of him. Putting out his hands, he felt
that it was the door. Coughing to try to clear his lungs,
he stood on shaky legs and tried to open it enough to
get out, but it wouldn't budge. Something was blocking it.

He slammed his body against the door, but it barely
moved. He slammed into it again, with all his weight
this time, and it flew open. Caught by surprise, he
stumbled and fell. Sprawling face first, he gasped for
air, but the smoke from the burning brush brought
new fits of coughing. He had to get out of there.

Hauling himself to his hands and knees, he heard a
grinding noise behind him and turned in time to see a

landslide rushing downhill toward him. He didn't even have time to say "Oh shit!" before he was smashed into unconsciousness.

20

At the Control Complex—24 November

The surviving Brazilian infantry were in headlong flight from the smoking ruins of the small hill in the jungle by the time the laser finally stopped firing. Their own Finger of God had been pointed at them, and any man in his right mind feared its searing touch.

When the firing broke off, Ashley looked back at the complex, her bloodstained left arm hanging limp at her side and silent tears streaking her cheeks. She had taken a round through the shoulder but had not stopped to even check the bleeding.

Fires raged in the trees and undergrowth surrounding the bottom of the hill. Through the pall of smoke and flame she could see that the rocks at the rim of the crater marking the top of the hill glowed dull red where the laser had touched them. The entire top of the hill had been blasted away, and Alex was somewhere under the rubble.

"Can I call for help now?" Ash's voice was soft and vulnerable.

Kat's face was grim. "If you don't, Ash, I will. All he said was to get you out of there while he did what he had to do. He didn't say anything about not letting you go back in after it was all over.''

"Can you please call for me?''

Kat keyed her mike implant and made the call back to force headquarters.

While they waited for the planes to arrive, Kat checked Ashley's wound, covered it with a field bandage and put the arm in a sling. It was not life threatening, but it was serious enough to require hospitalization when they got back. She knew better, however, than to try to get Ash to take her morphine, sit back and wait for the Dustoff like a good girl. As long as Rosemont was unaccounted for, she'd stay on her feet one way or the other.

A Tilt Wing gunship diverted from another mission was the first aircraft on the scene. Ash immediately got in contact with the pilot and ordered him to use his rotor blast to blow out the fires that were raging in the brush so they could get back to the hill.

The Tilt Wing swooped down and came to a hover over the edge of the fire. The down blast from its rotors blew the flames out and sent a billowing cloud of smoke and ashes into the air. "Is that what you had in mind, Bold Strider?'' the pilot asked.

"That's most affirm,'' Ash sent back. "Now march it up to the hill and clear a path for us to that area I indicated.''

The Tilt Wing slowly moved forward, and as it moved, the rotor blast blew out the fire. Their helmet filters dropped for protection against the acrid smoke and the cloud of ashes thrown up by the rotor blast,

Ash, Kat and the grunts followed in its wake. The camouflaged door was hanging open when they reached it, but Rosemont wasn't anywhere around.

A gust of wind blew more smoke away, and he could barely be seen under the pile of rocks that had cascaded down on top of him when he had opened the stuck door.

"Alex!" Ash cried, and dashed forward. Dropping her rifle, she knelt beside him and started clawing at the rocks with her good hand. "Get a Dustoff in here!" she shouted. "Quick!"

"It's on the way, Ash." Kat dropped down beside her to help dig Rosemont out of the rubble. "I already called one for you."

WHEN ROSEMONT AWOKE, he found himself in a hospital room hooked up to a biomonitor and an IV drip bag. A quick inventory showed that his arms and legs were still attached, although his left leg was encased in an inflatable cast and his head was bandaged. More importantly, though, his male equipment was still intact.

In the bed next to him, Ashley was sleeping peacefully, a bandage showing on her left upper arm and shoulder. Relief shot through him; she had made it. He just hoped that Kat had come through, as well.

He was reaching for the button to summon the nurse when the door popped opened and Major Pavel Zerinski marched in. As always, the Russian's carefully tailored uniform was immaculate, and he wore it with the flair of an early-twentieth-century Czarist court dandy.

"Alex, my friend," he called. "I am glad to see you looking so good. From what I have heard of your exploits, you were badly hurt."

"I don't know," he said honestly. "I just woke up. The last I remember, I was opening the door to get out of that hill when the roof fell in on me. I don't even know what day it is."

"You were brought in yesterday."

"Jesus," he said. "Time flies when you're having fun. And speaking of fun, I'm sorry that I don't have any vodka to offer you. It's all back at my CP."

"Never to mind," Zerinski said with a laugh. "I brought enough for both of us."

He reached his hand into his side pants pocket and came out with a silver pocket flask engraved with the Russian Peacekeeper insignia. Opening the top, he handed it to Rosemont.

The company commander took the flask and drank deeply. "What's the situation out there?" he asked as he handed the flask back.

Zerinski shrugged after taking a drink. "Oh, it's all over. It ended the day you found that control center. We finished up our operation the same afternoon."

"But what happened?"

He grinned broadly. "We just dropped in on the Argentinean launch sites and stopped them from firing their nuclear missiles."

"Just like that?"

"Well…we did have to persuade them a little. They had a full brigade guarding the launch sites and they unwisely decided to argue with us for a while."

Rosemont knew the penchant for understatement shared by all field commanders, the almost mandatory playing things down so as not to appear to be bragging. He also knew that it had not been as easy as Zerinski was making it out to have been. "How long did it take?" he asked.

The Russian's face clouded for a short moment. "It took me, the Second Company and the aviation company a day and a half. We destroyed the brigade, as well as the TASA armored battalion they sent to reinforce it."

"That sounds like you guys got into quite a pissing contest."

"It was." Zerinski's eyes showed that he was remembering a bitter fight. "But it will be a long time before they try anything like that again. We are occupying their capital and dismantling their military forces. The Triple Alliance of South America is no more. The UN has rounded up all the Argentineans responsible for their nuclear-weapons program, and there will be a public trial."

The Russian shook his head. "I do not know what it takes to convince these people that we Peacekeepers simply will not allow nuclear weapons to be used again."

Ashley had woken up in time to hear Zerinski's last statement. "War! War! War!" she chanted softly.

Zerinski spun around at the sound of her voice. "Ah," he said, bowing low at the waist. "Captain Ashley, I'm so glad you could join us."

She winced as she rolled over and sat up. Her left shoulder and upper arm were in bandages. "Good to see you, Pavel, I'm glad you made it through this rat fuck."

"I am glad you did, as well," Zerinski said. "In fact, as soon as you can leave here, the officers of the Third Company would be honored to have you as our guest for several days. And—" he bowed deeply "—I would be happy to act as your personal escort."

"I appreciate the invitation." She smiled and looked directly at Rosemont. "But you'd better talk to my fiancé about that."

Zerinski's eyes flicked back to Rosemont. "Oh..." For once he was openmouthed and at a complete loss for words. "I didn't know," he finally said. "Congratulations."

"Thank you," Rosemont replied, a rather puzzled look on his face. "I didn't know, either."

Zerinski was confused for a moment until he realized what was going on. Apparently the strong-willed Ashley Wells had struck again. Oh well, there was still Tanya, the new subaltern in the antitank platoon. He hadn't tried his luck with her yet.

AN HOUR LATER Rosemont was awakened from a deep sleep by a metallic grating noise. Sitting up in his bed, he leaned forward and listened intently. He heard nothing except for the ordinary hospital sounds he had grown accustomed to. He glanced over at Ashley, who was sleeping soundly, and he suppressed an urge to wake her. Lying back down, he gazed up unseeing at the ceiling and within minutes he had dozed off again.

A new sound brought him instantly awake, a sharp metallic clacking sound coming from the ward floor. Looking toward the door, he saw one of the deadly TASA mechanical cockroaches antipersonnel robot bombs scurrying across the floor toward him.

Rolling out of his bed, he grabbed his LAR and, quickly chambering a round, aimed at the metallic cockroach. The burst of 5 mm fire cut across the body of the robot, but it didn't detonate. Instead of the explosion he had expected to hear, he heard the sound of breaking glass and he was suddenly sprayed with a rank-smelling fluid. The spray arced out to cover the walls and ceiling.

"Outfuckingstanding, Rosemont," he heard Ashley say before she burst out in laughter.

Spinning around, he looked at her as if she had lost her mind. She was laughing so hard that tears were rolling down her cheeks. Unable to speak, she was pointing her finger at the destroyed robot. As the adrenaline started to wear off, he picked up the overwhelming aroma of the liquid that now covered the room and saw the bouquet of flowers on the robot's sensor turret.

Comprehension dawned on him, and his knees gave way. He dropped onto the floor and howled with laughter. "Champagne! It's that fucking Zerinski again!"

The ward nurse who had come running into the room at the sound of gunfire stood speechless as Zerinski brushed past her, a control box for the robot in his hand.

"Well," the Russian said. "I can see you that you two are not quite well enough to appreciate a delicacy like Russian champagne. But, as always, I am prepared for all emergencies," he said, pulling out his silver flask and three shot glasses. "How about some brandy?"

This sent Rosemont and Ashley into uncontrollable laughter again. The nurse pushed past Zerinski and demanded to know what was going on.

Zerinski turned toward her and bowed gracefully. "It is, how do you say, madam, 'happy hour'? My friends and I are preparing to celebrate all we have done to make this poor world a safer place to live."

The woman's nostrils flared as she became aware of the overpowering smell, and her eyes surveyed the room for the first time, taking in the broken glass littering the floor around the blasted robot. "I want to know what in the hell is going on here."

"As I explained, madam," he said, taking her arm and firmly steering her toward the door. "We are about to enjoy ourselves, and may I suggest you return to you duties."

"But this place smells like a brewery, and you're all drunk. I will not permit this."

Zerinski bellowed with laughter and gently shoved her through the door. "We are not drunk, madam, I can assure you of that. Not yet, at least." He shut the door in her protesting face.

Turning back to Ashley and Rosemont, he handed them each a shot glass and filled them to the top with the amber-colored liquid. "Since you completely destroyed what I thought was a rather clever little gift, all I have to share is what little I have left of my own private stock here."

Ashley snorted as she eyed her drink. "That smells more like USEF-issue booze to me, Pavel, but it'll do. I'm not fussy."

She raised her glass to the two men standing by her bed. "To the men and women of the American and Russian peacekeeping forces," she said. "May we never run out of something to drink. Saving the world is thirsty work."

Rosemont and Zerinski raised their glasses together. "Hear, hear."

When she had downed her drink, Ashley started chanting the Peacekeepers' battle cry, "War! War! War."

Rosemont immediately joined in. "War! War! War!"

As soon as Zerinski realized what they were saying, he also joined in. "War! War! War!"

Their chant was joined by the other wounded Peacekeepers in the ward, and Rosemont locked eyes with his wounded woman warrior. It was an imperfect world they lived in, but he had finally found someone who would fight at his side when he tried to correct these imperfections. That made his personal world perfect.

"War! War! War!" rose the chorus around them.

**In the battlefield of covert warfare America's toughest
agents play with lethal precision in the third installment of**

SLAM

by DAN MATTHEWS

In Book 3: SHADOW WARRIORS, hostile Middle East leaders
are using the drug pipeline to raise cash for a devastating nuclear arsenal and the SLAM commando unit is ordered to dis-
mantle the pipeline, piece by piece.

Inner-city hell just found a new savior—

JAKE STRAIT

BOGEYMAN

by FRANK RICH

Jake Strait is hired to infiltrate a religious sect in Book 3: **DAY OF JUDGMENT**. Hired to turn the sect's team of bumbling soldiers into a hit squad, he plans to lead the attack against the city's criminal subculture.

Jake Strait is a licensed enforcer in a future world gone mad—a world where suburbs are guarded and farmlands are garrisoned around a city of evil.

A struggle for survival in
a savage new world.

JAMES AXLER

DEATH LANDS.

Deep Empire

The crystal waters of the Florida Keys have turned into a death
zone. Ryan Cawdor, along with his band of warrior survivalists,
has found a slice of heaven in this ocean hell—or has he?

Welcome to the Deathlands, and the future nobody planned for.